Born in Edinburgh in 1906, **John Innes Mackintosh Stewart** was educated at Oriel College, Oxford, where he was presented with the Matthew Arnold Memorial Prize and named a Bishop Frazer's scholar. After graduation he went to Vienna to study Freudian psychoanalysis for a year.

His first book, an edition of Florio's translation of *Montaigne*, got him a lectureship at the University of Leeds. In later years he taught at the universities of Adelaide, Belfast and Oxford.

Under his pseudonym, Michael Innes, he wrote a highly successful series of mystery stories. His most famous character is John Appleby, who inspired a penchant for donnish detective fiction that lasts to this day. His other well-known character is Honeybath, the painter and rather reluctant detective, who first appeared in *The Mysterious Commission*, in 1975.

Stewart's last novel, *Appleby and the Ospreys*, appeared in 1986. He died aged eighty-eight.

D1649527

MICHAEL INNES

A CHANGE OF HEIR

HOUSE OF
STRATUS

This edition published in 2001 by House of Stratus, an imprint of Stratus Books Ltd, 21 Beeching Park, Kelly Bray, Cornwall, PL17 8QS, UK.

www.houseofstratus.com

Typeset, printed and bound by House of Stratus.

A catalogue record for this book is available from the British Library and the Library of Congress.

ISBN 1-84232-727-5
EAN 978-184232-545-2

PART ONE

PROLOGUE IN SOUTH KENSINGTON

1

ON HER MAJESTY'S SERVICE
OFFICIAL PAID
INLAND REVENUE

The buff-coloured card lay forbiddingly on George Gadberry's sketchy breakfast-table. Although well accustomed to the receipt of these vexatious applications, Gadberry still felt a little frightened – as well as alerted and wary – whenever he received one. They represented a side of life that he wasn't, somehow, terribly good at. Why, he asked himself as he eyed this particular specimen, shouldn't *he* be 'official paid'? There would be some sense in that. The theatrical profession was of inestimable benefit to the cultural life of the community, but it was undeniably overcrowded. One did the devil of a lot of 'resting', as it was ironically called. He himself had been taking this dubious kind of ease longer than he cared to count. There had been that delusive success in *The Rubbish Dump* and really quite a lot of money. Then there had been a couple of flops, followed by nothing at all. Now here he was. Yes, he ought certainly to be 'official paid', whether working or not. You could bet that the chap who sent out these nasty little missives was. Probably he got through the job in a couple of mornings weekly, and put in the rest of his office hours at dominoes or some equally squalid recreation.

Gadberry walked over to the window and surveyed some of South London's chimney pots. The prospect – urban, yet detectably autumnal – presented nothing to fortify or inspire. He went back to the table and flicked the card over on its other side. It was pretty well the same hue, he noticed, as the stains on the cloth provided by Mrs Lapin. He let his eye, for a start, travel only round its periphery. Bottom right, it said in very small print:

Wt 43085/M6195 WH & S 712/21.

Bottom left, it was snappier and the print bolder:

No. 145A.

Top left – for he was going round clockwise – it said, rather uninventively:

HM INSPECTOR OF TAXES

Top right had:

PLEASE QUOTE 16288D

Gadberry found himself speculating about that 'D'. He guessed it was pretty special to himself. Perhaps it stood for *Desperate Character*. More probably it stood for *Dodger*. Unless, indeed, it was rather technical, in which case the word might be *Drifter*. He was a drifter rather than a dodger, he supposed. It was the less active occupation.

Suddenly very depressed, Gadberry allowed himself to drift – for it was precisely that – round the room. Mrs Lapin, he reflected, must at one time have taken a vigorous interest in the graphic arts. Where her walls weren't clothed with framed photographs of theatrical celebrities (all with the appearance of bearing exuberant signatures) they displayed sepia-toned reproductions of masterpieces of Victorian painting. Mrs Lapin's favourite themes were romantic courtship and rural seclusion. In several of the pictures these were resourcefully combined. But for some years Mrs Lapin's aesthetic responses seemed to have been in eclipse, for all these pleasing scenes were so dusty and fly-blown that their finer points were inaccessible to inspection.

Gadberry peered gloomily at the largest of the pictures. It represented a gentleman in eighteenth-century costume making a proposal of marriage to a young gentlewoman. He had chosen, suitably enough, a walled garden for the enterprise, and he had brought a whole pack of hounds with him to support him in his suit. The sagacious creatures were sniffing peacefully at the hollyhocks.

The young gentlewoman was sniffing bashfully at a rose. Finding no encouragement in this, Gadberry had recourse to another of the arts. He whistled the first eight notes of the Fifth Symphony. He squared his shoulders, twice repeated this musical performance, and walked back to the table.

> HM Inspector of Taxes requests an
> early reply to his communication of 23.11.64

That was all – and to the uninitiate it mightn't have seemed alarming. But George Gadberry knew his onions. He picked up the card distastefully from the table and placed it on a plate from which he had lately consumed a disagreeable species of porridge. He set a match to it, and watched the good work. As the card curled and blackened and the thin flame died away, Gadberry spoke aloud to the solitude of his attic room.

'It stinks,' he murmured. 'And I am ready to depart.'

He went over to the rickety wardrobe and lifted down his suitcase. It was disgracefully dusty, so he hauled one of Mrs Lapin's sheets from his unmade bed and cleaned it up a bit with that. He wouldn't be sleeping in this room again.

Of course – he told himself as he packed – it isn't actually a chap at all that sends out these beastly things. It's a kind of low-grade computer. (No doubt it plays dominoes, just the same.) That's why it can be defeated simply by keeping on moving on. This had been explained to him by persons more skilled in these matters than he was himself. The machine is untiring but it can't speed up. You can always keep just ahead of it. You can do this even while owning a sequence of those 'permanent addresses' necessary for the receipt of National Assistance. He had never, as it happened, had a go at National Assistance; it was obviously a confusing sort of business – and moreover his bourgeois ancestry left him obstinately persuaded that such a means of subsistence was – unless one was senile or otherwise incapable – a bit shaming, after all. He preferred a little money picked up from time to time in honest menial employment. Not, of course, that *he* was honest. He still had his bourgeois pride, but his bourgeois honesty was a luxury he'd been obliged to scrap – to scrap, that was to say, in various petty directions. It was very horrid. He didn't like it at all. But that was where the tides of society had, so to speak, drifted him. For example, he quite liked old Ma Lapin. He was sorry that circumstances made it impossible for him to take a formal leave of her. But circumstances, in the shape of ten days' board and lodging, unfortunately did. He'd go downstairs in his socks.

George Gadberry began on the Fifth Symphony again, but this time he stopped after the three little pips at the beginning. Sometimes he wondered if he was imagining things. About the low-grade computer, that was to say. Perhaps if he faced it he'd find that it wasn't disposed to bite really hard. It's only concern with him could be with the substantial dollop that had come in during the run of *The Rubbish Dump*, and that was now a depressingly long time ago. Perhaps the machine was anxious to make contact only to murmur something about a bad debt and calling it a day. He himself had almost certainly mismanaged the whole affair. More successful members of his profession, he knew, solved these small troubles by going in for a ploy known as a theatrical bankruptcy. Perhaps he'd gone wrong in not fixing himself something quite modest in that line.

He finished packing. It didn't take long. He counted his small change. That didn't take long either. It would be necessary, he saw, to find a friend on whom to park himself. To park himself, he would have to explain, while considering his position. He doubted whether he possessed a friend to whom that would sound very convincing. But he possessed several who, convinced or unconvinced, would be prepared to have him around for a while. This ought to be comforting. But the knowledge, somehow, didn't altogether please him. Being regarded as quite an agreeable character was, of course, itself agreeable. 'Rather endearing, really,' was what he imagined people were inclined to say about him. It was undeniably useful, making an impression like that. Nevertheless a consciousness of it seldom failed to kindle in him a small, obstinate spark of what was conceivably divine discontent. Unfortunately sparks of that order hadn't much utility. You couldn't as much as toast a bloater by them when the gas had been cut off.

Gadberry went downstairs very quietly. With any luck Ma Lapin would be in her own quarters in the basement. She was a lazy old soul, and didn't commonly get round to 'doing' her lodgers' rooms – when she 'did' them at all – until much later in the morning. He might, of course, run into one or another of the lodgers themselves. But that wouldn't greatly matter. Even if they guessed what he was up to they wouldn't give him away. He was on very good terms with the lot.

He did, in fact, encounter one of them. It was the girl in the second-floor back. She danced, if you could call it that, in some pretty low spot he'd forgotten the name of, and he just hadn't, somehow, been able to take the interest in her that she'd seemed to have in mind at one time. But she still wasn't unfriendly, he sensed, even although it was now her habit to toss up her chin and turn away whenever they met.

She did this on the present occasion – and so speedily that she probably hadn't even noticed the suitcase.

And then, in the hall, there was Bessie Lapin. He'd more or less expected that. The child seemed to lead much of her dismal existence there. Her hair was always in twists of grubby paper, her nose was always running, and her only occupation was sitting on the tiled floor, crooning or drooling over a battered doll. This was happening now.

'Hullo, Bessie! Is your mum around?'

Gadberry put this question heartily, and in the hope of getting a reassuring report that Mrs Lapin was indeed buried in her own lower regions. But Bessie offered no reply at all. She just stared dully at Gadberry, and sniffed. That Mrs Lapin was really her mum seemed wholly improbable. Bessie, poor kid, was certainly the child of heaven knew whom, and planted indefinitely here heaven knew why.

'Who lent thee, child, this meditative guise?' Gadberry asked. There was no particular reason why he should thus quote Matthew Arnold. It certainly wasn't with any notion of teasing Bessie. So he was mildly horrified to see a slow flush spread over her whole face – as it will spread over the face of an adult who has been deeply mortified. He grabbed the handle of the front door and got outside quick.

He'd made good his escape. But halfway down the grubby flight of steps leading to the pavement he paused, frowning. It might even have been said that he paused, scowling. Then he turned round and re-entered the hall, put down the suitcase, and fumbled in a trouser-pocket. He held out a sixpence to the child, who got nimbly to her feet as he did so.

'Bessie,' he said, 'you run out and buy yourself a lolly.'

Bessie advanced, snatched the coin, retreated rapidly, and edged round towards the open door while keeping as much distance between Gadberry and herself as possible. She displayed no more gratitude than one might expect from some small anthropoid creature at the zoo.

'Mr Gadberry – is that you?'

Gadberry turned round and faced disaster. The door shutting off the basement staircase had opened, and Ma Lapin stood in it. She looked curiously at the suitcase and appeared to be about to animadvert upon it. Then her immediate business with her lodger recurred to her.

'Telephone,' she said. 'It's an agency.'

'The St James's?' It was with a proper lack of excitement that Gadberry asked this. But his heart had given a bound. An engagement, even of an insignificant sort, would solve some immediate problems very nicely.

'No. Something I never heard of. The Bernhardt. Party of the name of Falsetto.'

'Ah, yes. Well, I'll have a word with him.' Gadberry, who was a little dashed, moved with dignity – but not too tardy a dignity – towards

Mrs Lapin's staircase. The only telephone of which the establishment boasted was in the basement – an arrangement which might be presumed to afford Mrs Lapin valuable insights into the lives of her lodgers. 'Falsetto is quite an enterprising chap,' he said – skirting, so to speak, Mrs Lapin's back quarters on the way to her lower ones. 'I've let him fix things up for me from time to time.'

Mrs Lapin made no reply. Her glance had returned to the suitcase. Gadberry remembered with relief that he'd locked it. Ma Lapin, of course, might go up and take a look at his room. But by the time she had wheezed her way up there and down again, there was a good chance that he would have concluded his business with Falsetto and beaten it. This, indeed, might well be in Ma Lapin's mind now.

He made his way to the telephone and picked up the receiver.

2

'George – yes?'

'Yes – George.' Gadberry wasn't aware that he'd ever given Mr Falsetto permission to *George* him. In fact he resented it. But then, despite his necessarily Bohemian life, he frequently found himself resenting things that would have been judged censurable either in the vicarage in which he had been born or in the school at which he had been educated. Such resentments weren't much good when you had just reduced your capital assets by sixpence and knew that they now stood at eight shillings. 'Nice of you to call me,' Gadberry said firmly. This *George* business, after all, might be of good omen. Perhaps Peter Hall had been showing interest. Perhaps the author of *The Rubbish Dump* was out of jail and had written another play. Gadberry tried to remember Mr Falsetto's Christian name, and had to decide that it had never been communicated to him. Perhaps it might be possible to take a guess at it. If one were unfortunate enough to be a Falsetto, what would it occur to one to call one's darling boy? Well, there were Scottish names almost as outlandish: Colkitto and Patullo, for instance. So one might dower him with an ancient Scottish lineage by calling him Donald or Dugald. Gadberry decided to try one of these. 'Dugald, old boy,' he said, 'you've got a show for me?'

'Falsetto here.'

'Yes, I know.' Gadberry, although anxious to get down to business, wasn't going to be put off. 'Old boy,' he reiterated chattily, 'you have the advantage of me. In this business of names I mean. What do your intimates call you?'

'Intimates?' Mr Falsetto sounded suspicious and offended. 'You kidding? I'm a family man.'

'Yes, of course.' Gadberry had been rather pleased with his turn of phrase, which he recalled as having been used by his father. But it had set Mr Falsetto on a wrong track. 'I mean, old boy, what's your Christian name? If you're to call me – '

'Christian name?' Mr Falsetto's voice conveyed a kind of blank interrogation. The concept appeared to be one with which he could do nothing.

'*First* name. *Given* name. The kind of name you're naming when you call me George.'

'Okay, okay. I get. Norval. My name is Norval. You call me that.'

'Thank you. I'd like to.'

Gadberry was naturally pleased that his guess had been within the target area. Now he could get down to brass tacks. 'Norval, old chap,' he said, 'what's the show? What's the part? Spill it. I can take it.'

'Search me, George. But you go to see this Smith.'

'Smith?'

'Sure. John Smith. Now – at the Chester Court. That's a hotel somewhere Kensington way, I guess.'

'What's this Smith – an impresario?'

'I'd say not, George. Not with that name. And not in that hotel.'

'Then why – '

'Better call him a client, I guess. He paid my fee, and that makes him a client, don't it? And then he went through all the files. Only I reckon it was only the photographs he was interested in. He wasn't really digging the text.'

'But that's absurd!' Gadberry was indignant. 'You don't think I'm going to go modelling, do you – posing in somebody's raincoat or light summer suiting beside a lion in Trafalgar Square?'

'I can't say, George. It's over to you.'

'That's the sort of thing this Smith must want, isn't it? It's the only thing makes them choose just like that. And, after all, I *am* an actor, Norval. Can't you do a bit better – '

'George, here's this thing on my desk talking at me. My secretary says Sir Laurence – '

'All right, Norval.' Gadberry had no belief in Sir Laurence. 'But just tell me what this man Smith *said*.'

'Said? Well, I figure he didn't kind of say much. Except that you were the nearest thing to his type he'd turned up. George, I'll be seeing you sometime.'

'Stop, Dugald! I mean Norval.' Gadberry was reduced to a frank betrayal of agitation. 'Would you say this fellow Smith was a – '

'The Chester Court, George. You can find out for yourself, easy enough. Only let me know if it's something not quite nice. The Bernhardt is a very strictly ethical concern. That's how I started it in New York, and that's how I've continued it over here.'

'I'm sure it is.' Fleetingly, Gadberry wondered why, if this were so, Mr Falsetto appeared to be resigned to an expatriate condition. 'But what's the chap *like*? At least tell me that.'

'Like, George? Well, I'd say he's like any other guy in dark glasses and a beard. So long, George.'

'But look here – ' A click on the line constrained Gadberry to break off. Whether for the purpose of receiving Sir Laurence or not, Mr Norval Falsetto had put down his telephone.

Gadberry went thoughtfully upstairs again. With Mr Falsetto, he supposed, anybody became George – or Richard or Robert, as the case might be – on the occasion of his having brought the Bernhardt a fee. He recalled that it had been with some misgiving that he had placed himself on the Bernhardt's register. He'd had more than an inkling of its being something which, in the higher ranges of his profession, just wasn't all that frequently done. And Mr John Smith of the beard and the dark glasses didn't sound attractive; in fact he spoke loudly of an unattractiveness so pronounced that it remained exactly that even when viewed from the standpoint of a highly disagreeable indigence. He probably wanted to command, for a modest fee, some boring and senseless service. He might yearn, for example, while bizarrely attired and to the accompaniment of the music of Wagner, to be bitten or beaten or bashed about by a young man of personable appearance.

These and other morbid hypotheses were abruptly banished from Gadberry's mind by the consciousness that he was once more in the presence of Mrs Lapin. As he had guessed would happen, she hadn't stirred out of the hall. Nor had Bessie; the child had simply retreated to a corner and turned on her drooling act. The compromising suitcase formed a centrepiece to the composition.

'Well,' Gadberry said briskly, 'Falsetto sounds as if he may have something attractive. But I don't want to be in a hurry. There's talk of taking *The Rubbish Dump* to Moscow. Of course I'd be needed for that.'

'A good riddance, if you ask me. Clean crazy, plays of that sort are.' Ma Lapin folded her arms across her bosom; it was clear that she was in one of her nasty moods. 'Theatres of cruelty, theatres of the absurd! Who ever heard of such things in old Cocky's time? That Lord Chamberpot ought to come down on them heavy. That's what I say.'

Bessie Lapin began to cry – whether nostalgically at the mention of C B Cochran or in terror at the thought of the Lord Chamberpot, it was impossible to say.

'Well, well,' Gadberry said cheerily, 'we all have our tastes and fancies, Mrs Lapin.' He frowned as he recalled the probability that precisely this reflection might be applied in charity, no doubt, to Mr John Smith. But Mr John Smith was neither here nor there. There could be no question of his seeking out so shady a character at the Chester Court or anywhere else. Gadberry advanced resolutely upon his suitcase. 'And now,' he said, 'I'd better be getting along.' He caught Mrs Lapin's eye. 'For the time being, that is,' he added rather obscurely.

'Do I understand, Mr Gadberry, that you are leaving us for some days?' Mrs Lapin had shifted her position. In fact she was now planted in front of the door which would lead her lodger to freedom. 'Perhaps a country-house weekend with the aristocracy? Or a professional engagement at Chequers, it might be? Mr George

Gadberry gives his celebrated farmyard imitations to the assembled Prime Ministers of the Empire?'

'Nothing of the sort, Mrs Lapin.' Gadberry contrived the appearance of taking these crude jibes as sallies of refined wit. He was not, of course, in the habit of offering farmyard imitations; it was a form of the mimetic art, he supposed, that had retreated from the music hall to the village institute round about the time that he was born. Mrs Lapin herself, it occurred to him, could put up a very fair show as an enraged turkey. But this was all the more reason for speaking her fair. 'As a matter of fact,' he said, 'I expect to be back by lunch time.' He picked up the suitcase – contriving, as he did so, a great appearance of its being as light as a feather. 'I'm simply taking a few things round to the cleaner's. Rather a grubby part of London, this.' He saw that here was an unhappy remark, for Ma Lapin was showing signs of mounting truculence. 'No offence intended,' he added hastily.

' 'E give me a tanner!' Quite unexpectedly, Bessie Lapin had thrust out a pointing finger at Gadberry. Both her gesture and her tone were of an accusatory nature. The child might have been saying ' 'e give me a clip on the ear', or even 'Ma, e did something rude'. There was a moment's silence. ' 'E give me a tanner to buy a lolly, 'e did,' Bessie elaborated with undiminished severity. She held up the coin as if it were some damning piece of evidence.

'Well, that was very kind of Mr Gadberry, I'm sure.' Ma Lapin's expression had softened. 'A very nice thought.' She moved away from the door, looking straight at Gadberry as she did so. 'But we mustn't keep you,' she said. 'You'll be wanting to get to the cleaner's before the rush. Bessie, open the door for Mr Gadberry.'

Bessie did as she was told. Gadberry gave the suitcase a jaunty swing, because it was more or less automatic with him to keep up a bit of acting once he had embarked upon it. In actuality, he noticed, it was surprisingly heavy. But this, he knew, wasn't why he was a little flushed as he passed through the doorway and made his way into the liberty of the street. Being rather more than normally quick in such matters, he had understood that straight look of Ma Lapin's in a flash. Of course she hadn't been for a moment taken in as to what he was about. Come to think of it, no experienced theatrical landlady could have been. It was simply that the blessed sixpence – or was it the damned sixpence? – had tipped some balance in her mind. She had seen him as a poor devil who was down and out, and she had let him go.

Gadberry walked off down the nearly deserted side street. He walked surprisingly quickly, considering the burden he was carrying. This was partly a matter of prudence – the odd old girl might change her mind – and partly because he was bitterly and mysteriously angry. He supposed he was angry with a world that had of late been treating him so scurvily. But he was in no doubt that he was angry with himself as well. The two emotions seemed simultaneously to combine and to conflict. The resulting state of mind was extremely uncomfortable.

He found a telephone kiosk, set down his suitcase where it would be safely in view, and went inside. He made one call which produced no answer, so that he pressed the button and got his money back. He made a second call, and got through, but the resulting conversation was unsatisfactory. He searched round in his head, and made two further calls: the result of one might have been termed inconclusive and embarrassing, and the result of the other came rapidly and unmistakably. He counted his money. These beastly machines had become horribly expensive to operate. He decided to give up. There was a woman waiting impatiently to take his place, and he had an irrational feeling that she knew exactly the humiliating sort of sponging act he'd been engaged on.

He came out of the kiosk, and sat down on the suitcase. This action surprised and even a little frightened him. It was like walking in the gutter. If he just had a few boxes of matches to peddle he would make a perfectly ordinary sort of beggar, engaged in dodging the GLC's regulations against mendicancy. He found himself wishing that he was either very much younger or very much older. A twelve-year-old waif or stray is an honestly pathetic sort of spectacle. An old, old man in destitution has considerable scope for putting on a turn of marked dignity. Gadberry's mind wandered, and he found himself wondering whether he could play the part of the Leech Gatherer in a dramatisation of Wordsworth's celebrated *Resolution and Independence*. Then he became aware that some children were staring at him. Simultaneously, he recalled that his own actual age was twenty-seven. That was the nastiest part of the whole situation. He was twenty-seven, rather tall, rather more than distinctly good-looking, and the possessor of what often seemed to be regarded as an attractive personality. Yet here he was.

He got to his feet. At least, he supposed, he had better find out. He picked up the suitcase and made his way – rather trudgingly, now – to the Underground Station at Waterloo. Charing Cross, he supposed, and then change to the Central Line. He put down his last intact florin before the booking clerk.

'South Kensington, please,' he said.

3

The Chester Court was probably quite an expensive hotel. But what you got for your money there, Gadberry judged, wouldn't be likely to make much personal appeal to him. It was what elderly people called a 'quiet' hotel. No doubt it was 'old-established' too. The quietness was something to which you could have taken a knife; there was a large gloomy lounge in which, although it was sparsely populated, you couldn't imagine anybody speaking in more than a confidential whisper. The old-established effect was secured by ingeniously providing the smell of dust without the appearance of it; the stuff must have been buried deep in the curtains and upholstery. There were a good many palms in pots, and a good many of those rubber trees which, entirely fashionable a few years ago, were now sinking gently in the social scale, so that they were no doubt destined eventually to replace the aspidistra as the sacred emblem of the simplest classes of English society.

Gadberry had some leisure for making these sociological observations while he waited for Mr John Smith, who seemed in no hurry to appear. The Chester Court, incidentally, seemed an unlikely haunt for a person of dubious habits or inclinations. Gadberry drew a certain encouragement from this; perhaps Smith's proposals would be merely eccentric rather than pathological. Quite a number of the old parties sitting round this lounge undoubtedly harboured one or another of the milder lunacies of senescence. In one corner, for example, there was a garishly dressed elderly female who appeared to insist on carrying a canary round with her in a cage. In another a silver-haired man was delivering himself of a public speech without making any sound at all; you just knew it was a public speech by the eloquent gestures that accompanied it. You could tell that both these people were rather more than just prosperous. Perhaps Mr Smith belonged to the same harmless, pathetic but agreeably solvent world.

And here he was – beard, dark glasses and all. He was coming downstairs with a tread that showed him to be a good deal younger than anybody else in the place. He had on a light overcoat, and he was carrying a suitcase. Gadberry, whose own suitcase was still planted beside him, was struck by this circumstance at once. The direction of Smith's glance being indetectable, it wasn't possible to tell whether he had as yet spotted his visitor. Certainly he didn't come straight in Gadberry's direction. He went over to a desk saying 'Reception' and entered into some negotiation with the person in charge of it. In a moment it became quite clear that he was paying his bill. Gadberry watched this proceeding in some perplexity. He was also obscurely alarmed – so much so (although this was absurd) that he felt prompted to get up and bolt from the hotel. If Smith had booked in here only for the purpose of the present assignation it was pretty well a certainty that he was one sort of bad hat or another.

But Gadberry hesitated. He wasn't really very clear about his attitude to bad hats. He felt that there was a lot to be said for being anti-social. It was one's only way of protesting against the rotten way things were arranged. On the other hand it was difficult to be anti-social without at the same time being *anti* some more or less inoffensive individual chap. Even if you robbed a bank – which in itself would be an entirely laudable thing to do – you might find yourself hitting a perfectly nice man on the head, just to save your own skin. And there, Gadberry felt, you got into rather deep water. Nature red in tooth and claw, each man for himself, and so forth: he didn't seem ever to have worked these things out. He'd got along indifferently well – or ill – without much in the way of agonising appraisal in that sort of territory.

Smith was now moving towards the front door of the hotel, and for a moment Gadberry supposed that he was going to be ignored altogether. But then Smith made a detour that took him just behind Gadberry's chair.

'Let's get out of this,' Smith murmured. 'Follow me.' He spoke as casually as if to an old friend. Without pausing, he walked straight out into the street.

Gadberry took up his own suitcase and followed. It didn't seem to him that Smith was a very high-class conspirator. For one thing, high-class conspirators don't think up names like John Smith. And this meeting had been arranged not without suspicious singularity – supposing there to be anybody around who was interested in such things. He himself had come in and asked for Mr Smith. Mr Smith had presumably been told he had a visitor; and this rather dim conspiratorial scene had followed. It was like something out of a bad spy story. But of course neither the woman at the reception-desk nor the porter near the door was very likely to have spies in mind, or to be taking the slightest interest in Mr Smith as he checked out.

Once on the pavement, Smith slackened his pace until Gadberry caught up with him. They turned a corner, and Smith spoke.

'That thing heavy?' He nodded his bearded visage to indicate Gadberry's suitcase. 'We haven't far to go.'

'Tolerably,' Gadberry said, rather shortly. He was beginning to think his treatment improperly unceremonious.

'Holds everything you possess, I suppose. But we'll soon settle all that.'

This time Gadberry said nothing at all. He was outraged that the person calling himself Smith should be in a position to offer this accurate conjecture. Smith must have had more conversation with Falsetto than Falsetto had reported. And Falsetto must have a more precise sense of Gadberry's depressed situation than he was entitled to.

'Do you mind?' Smith had stopped by the kerb and again jerked his head. This time it was towards the centre of the road, into which there was dug one of those subterraneous retreats which in London are labelled either 'MEN' or 'GENTLEMEN' according – one must suppose

– to the political complexion of the particular local council involved. 'Only a jiffy,' Smith added reassuringly. Suitcase and all, he walked across the road and vanished underground.

Gadberry found it hard not to be indignant. Smith might reasonably have been expected to give thought to a matter of this sort before quitting his hotel. Gadberry looked up and down the road. If there had been a bus to board he would have boarded it. But there wasn't. If he simply hurried away on foot – burdened still by this damned suitcase – Smith would emerge from his retirement in plenty of time to give pursuit. So Gadberry stayed put. For one thing, he was now pretty curious about Smith.

Some minutes went by, and Smith didn't reappear – although several other people bobbed up above ground and went about their business. Gadberry suddenly noticed that this particular convenience was of the commodious sort that has an entrance at each end. He hadn't been keeping an eye on the farther end. Perhaps Smith had come up that way and vanished. Perhaps the whole thing was some peculiarly pointless species of practical joke.

Now another man came up. He was in a dark suit, and was carrying a suitcase. Gadberry recognised the suitcase. Then – after a fashion – he recognised the man. It was Smith transformed. The dark glasses had vanished, and the beard had vanished also. Smith crossed to the pavement.

'Well, that's better!' he said cheerfully – very much, indeed, as if he had in fact achieved some physical ease. 'We can be getting along.'

They got along. As they did so, two perceptions, each disconcerting, came to Gadberry. The first was a matter of more or less professional observation. Smith wasn't newly shaved. He smelt faintly of a kind of spirit with which Gadberry was familiar. The beard had been a false beard of the sort that you can soak off in no time. Gadberry was disturbed that he had been so thick as not to spot this at once.

There was now something familiar about Smith. Gadberry felt that he had seen him before. This was the second disconcerting fact – and it was much *more* disconcerting than the first. It occurred to him that he had perhaps had some forgotten brush with Smith in the past, and that the circumstances had been such as to give Smith some sinister hold over him now. But this was a morbid notion, since Gadberry had never really had quite that sort of past.

'By the way,' Smith said – and his tone had an oddly throw-away quality that seemed habitual with him – 'my name's Comberford. Spelt with two *o*'s but the first part rhymes with "lumber". Nicholas Comberford.'

'My name's Gadberry,' Gadberry said. 'And it has never been anything else.'

'All right, all right! You needn't be arrogant about it. You never know, you know.' Smith or Comberford continued cheerfully vague. 'You might have to change your name tomorrow. And why not? I don't think Gadberry's much of a name. Entirely plebeian in origin, I'd imagine.'

'Look here – '

'All right, all right! I know you've had the education of a gentleman, and all that. It wouldn't be any good – would it? – if you *hadn't*. I'm just saying that if you did have to lose your name, Gadberry isn't much of a name to lose. That's reasonable, isn't it?'

'I don't at all see why I might have to change my name.'

'You might have a wealthy aunt with aristocratic connections. She might disapprove of your upstart father – '

'Look here, I didn't have – '

'I'm only putting a case, old chap. This wealthy aunt might leave you a fortune, on condition that you took her name. Cholmondeley, for instance, or Fetherstonhaugh, or – '

'I think this is a very stupid conversation.'

'So it is.' Nicholas Comberford nodded emphatically. 'It's about Gadberry, which I was saying is rather a stupid name.'

'It's a very old name.' Rather unexpectedly, Gadberry found himself concerned to vindicate his lineage. 'There was a Gadberry in the seventeenth century, if you want to know. Only he spelt it Gadbury, with a *u*.'

'And what did he do?'

'He was an astrologer, as a matter of fact. But right at the top of his profession.'

'You're not right at the top of yours, are you, Gadberry, old chap?'

Not unnaturally, this impertinence outraged Gadberry. It came into his head that he ought perhaps to hit Comberford on the jaw. But he doubted whether he could do this effectively without putting down his suitcase – and even, in common fairness, without inviting Comberford to do the same. This seemed awkwardly elaborate. Moreover it was dawning on Gadberry that conceivably he was taking rather a liking to this objectionable person. He didn't at all know why. Perhaps it was simply that, whatever the man was up to, it wasn't any of those boring and unacceptable proceedings that Gadberry had been envisaging. Moreover Comberford was a rogue. He couldn't but be a rogue. In fact he was a crook. Only crooks disguise or undisguise themselves in public lavatories. Gadberry was interested.

'At the top of my profession?' he repeated. 'Of course not. If I were, I wouldn't be taking up with a small-time conman like Nicholas Comberford. Would I, now?'

'Well, here we are.' Comberford had stopped before rather an imposing flight of steps. He didn't seem at all offended. 'It's not too bad. Same sort of place as the one we've come from, but a good deal classier. The old girl booked me into it, of course. She has classy tastes. Indeed, you might say she has a lavish sort of mind. Thinks big, as it were. Which, of course, is the key to the situation. Now, then – in we go.'

4

It was an obscurely fateful moment. Sensing this, George Gadberry hesitated. This second hotel, he noticed, was very much like the first. Round here there were scores of these respectable and colourless places. It was hard to associate them with anything that might be called dirty work. Yet he was now sure that the man calling himself Nicholas Comberford was a dangerous companion. He was attracted to him because he felt that they shared certain common assumptions. But they weren't, perhaps, very salubrious assumptions – so that his own prudent course, even at this late hour, would be to turn round and make a bolt for it. Unfortunately it *was* a late hour, if only in the sense that an impressive hall porter, followed by a subordinate functionary of the same sort, was coming down the steps with the evident intention of relieving Comberford and himself of their suitcases. The new hotel was evidently a plushy sort of place. Comberford, in addition to his less definable attractiveness, was clearly in on the gravy. Gadberry thought of the few remaining pennies and sixpences in his own pocket. The thought of Mrs Lapin, who had let him go and certainly wouldn't want to see him again. He handed over his suitcase and climbed the steps.

'The food,' Comberford said, 'is surprisingly good. I wonder if the old girl knew that? Anyway, there's time for a drink or two, and then we'll have a spot of lunch.' He turned and gave some direction to the hall porter, with the result that the suitcases were spirited away. 'I have my own sitting-room, as a matter of fact. Her mind works that way. Everything laid on. Convenient for our little chat, wouldn't you say? But first we'll just sit down here and have a spot. Waiter' – Comberford made a commanding gesture – 'two dry Martinis!'

Gadberry felt increasingly unnerved. Settling down in the corner of the lounge, and beneath the shade of palms luxuriant beyond the ambition of the Chester Court, he stole a good look at his companion. He was again visited by the disturbing sense that the man was familiar to him – disturbing because his memory, or seeming memory, was of somebody he rather liked but distinctly didn't trust. But who on earth could it be? The puzzle annoyed him, and annoyance prompted him to hostile speech.

'Look here,' he said, 'are you really being all that bright? You take a lot of trouble with false beards and noses and whatever, and then you haul me in here in the sight of the whole place. It doesn't make sense.'

'My dear man, it's perfectly all right. Nobody here will bother about us. The important thing was to leave a cold trail at that other place. It was the address, you know, that I gave your friend Falsetto. Not that anybody is going to get at Falsetto. Still, one can't be too careful. Not with the stakes as high as they are. Don't you agree? But here we're quite all right. A respectable resident, you might say, entertaining – well, entertaining his younger brother. Waiter – I don't think much of these as Martinis. Bring two more of the same size.'

This speech had an odd and powerful effect on Gadberry. For a moment he couldn't place it at all. He stared again at Comberford, and suddenly the truth came to him. The reference to a younger brother had revealed it. The person Comberford reminded him of was himself. They must indeed be almost as alike as identical twins. He'd been searching gropingly for the memory of somebody he rather liked and decidedly didn't trust. Of course that person was himself. It was a description that fitted him perfectly.

He took yet another look at Comberford, and saw that he was a distinctly handsome man. This was gratifying as far as it went. He saw too that 'identical twins' was a little wide of the mark. Comberford was older than he was – perhaps by eight, certainly by five years.

It was fantastic! The sense of being in a bizarre situation produced in Gadberry a renewed sense of alarm.

But it also attracted him, just as Comberford himself did. Sitting around Ma Lapin's, waiting for something that didn't happen, and waiting as often as not without even the price of a drink: this had made of late a pretty dull sort of life. It had made a duller life, certainly, than is at all tolerable at twenty-seven. So now he steadied himself by drinking his Martini – all at a go, since another was on the way – and addressed Comberford with at least a moderated hostility.

'I don't know what this is about,' he said. 'But aren't you taking a bloody lot for granted? You go to this chap Falsetto, and you rake through hundreds of photographs until you see something like your own face staring at you. It happens to be mine, and you know nothing about me. But you take it for granted that I can be hired for whatever funny business is in your head.'

'So you can, old boy.'

'I'll thank you not to call me "old boy".' Gadberry marked with satisfaction the arrival of the second round of Martinis. They prompted him, indeed, to a return to truculence. 'I have to bandy that stuff with Falsetto and his sort. But I'll be damned if I'll be old-boyed by you.'

'All right, George. I suppose I may call you George? For the time being, that is. It isn't much of a name, if you ask me. You could find a better one.'

'And I don't like this stupid talk about names. First about Gadberry, and then about George.' Gadberry took a gulp of his second Martini. 'Weren't you taught one doesn't make jokes about people's names?'

'That's fine, George!' There was genuine satisfaction in Comberford's voice. 'You had a nursery, hadn't you? And then a schoolroom, and then a prep school, and then Harrow or Rugby or whatever, after that? All the works, just as I had. And that's a great relief. You see, Falsetto's dossier – would it be called that? – didn't run to information of that kind. And it would be no good if you were some sort of jumped-up prole. The old girl simply wouldn't take it.'

'Who the devil is this old girl you keep on talking about?'

'Drink up, old boy. George, I mean. No heel-taps. And now we'll go up and have lunch.'

The lunch was a good one. To Gadberry, whose palate had of late been confined within the gastronomic range of Mrs Lapin, it seemed very good indeed. Comberford, however, pronounced it no more than modestly meritorious. It would be at about the level, he supposed, of what the 'old girl' put up with at home, and no doubt she came here for the same thing when she had to visit London. It was a bit pathetic, surely, just not knowing what you could command if you wanted to. Still, although she was as old as the hills, she was not perhaps beyond the reach of education in these and other matters.

Gadberry listened to these remarks for the most part in silence. He naturally found Comberford's oblique manner of approaching whatever it was he had to propose more than a little irritating. Who the 'old girl' was simply hadn't so far appeared, although it seemed a reasonable guess that she was some rich and eccentric relative. Certainly riches were well in the centre of the picture; they were the first element, so to speak, to take solid form through the haze of Comberford's random and elusive talk. Gadberry saw that there was a certain cleverness in this sort of softening-up process; he was being edged into a mood of suspense and irritated curiosity. Of course something disreputable was going to be proposed to him. Of this there could be no doubt. It would almost certainly be a thoroughly predatory plan, with those carefully emphasised riches for quarry.

Gadberry found that he had coffee and brandy before him, and that he was smoking a highly agreeable cigar. He withdrew his attention from Comberford for a time – the man seemed not ready to come to the point – in order to consider these pleasures soberly. Casting Comberford in the role of a Mephistopheles and himself in that of Dr Faustus, he tried to decide for just how many cigars and just how many brandies he would be prepared to do just what. But the equation, he found, had no real meaning. Cigars were all right in themselves, but he certainly wouldn't risk much in the way of trouble in return for a lifetime's supply. But change a box of cigars magically into a hareem of houris – and what then? He suspected he didn't know. On the large speculative issue of Everything-that-money-can-buy he didn't really have a clue. He had been brought up to believe that the quest of riches is ignoble and delusory. For all he knew, this pious conclusion might be precisely true.

But Gadberry was much clearer about penury. Pious praise of poverty, at least, was poppycock. The ability to command this and that might ultimately prove pretty futile. But the *inability* to do the same thing was something he was fairly confident there was little to be said for. And particularly in the simple world of modest satisfactions: beer, if not brandy; fags if not cigars.

> *Happy the man whose wish and care*
> *A few paternal acres bound…*

Alexander Pope had been right, and that happy man – Gadberry felt – could be him. Only, the little plot of ground had never come his way, whether paternally or otherwise.

Further examined in the context of the Mephistopheles idea, all this perhaps led to the conclusion that he was prepared for mild turpitude for the sake of small gains. Put that way, it sounded more than a shade inglorious. Nor did it seem to fit the present situation – not with Comberford talking mysteriously of high stakes or whatever.

'For a start, I'd say, one ought to be clear about the theory of the thing. Wouldn't you agree?'

Gadberry turned his attention back to Comberford with a jerk. It sounded as if the man had at last said something definite – and while he himself had been doing this wool-gathering.

'Theory of what?' Gadberry asked. He tried to speak in his best tough and grudging manner. But the Martinis and the hock – for there had been hock – and the brandy had undoubtedly been doing a bit of a job. It might have been premature to say that he was feeling co-operative, but he could fairly have been described as approachable.

'The theory of what I've been talking about, George. Imposture, and so forth.'

Gadberry was almost certain that Comberford hadn't been talking about anything of the sort. It was just that he had this technique of assuming that you were more in the picture than you were.

'Imposture and impersonation,' Comberford amplified. 'My idea is that *il n'y a que le premier pas qui coûte.* You follow me? Only get off to a flying start and – '

'They did teach me a certain amount of French,' Gadberry said with some indignation. 'And no doubt you're right.'

'Once let suspicion stir, and nine-tenths of the battle is lost. So it's a tremendous challenge. Fortunately, George, you do have – I can see that you have – a fairly rapid sort of cunning. Would you agree?'

Gadberry didn't feel constrained to agree. The tribute struck him as of a disobliging sort. If it was true – and he believed it was – that his mind did move with a tolerable speed, he had better get it so moving now. Comberford had conducted this affair at his own pace for long enough.

'I think you said something about imposture and impersonation,' he began. 'Do you want me to impersonate you, or a younger brother of yours, or what?'

'Me. Of course I can see that you're a little younger than I am. But there will be nothing awkward about that. In fact, it may be psychologically advantageous. You'll see.'

'Is this just on one specific occasion?'

'Good Lord, no! I'm not proposing, my dear George, to waste your time in perpetrating some mere practical joke. It's nothing like that. Nothing like that, at all.'

'For how long, then?'

'Well, for quite a time.' Comberford hesitated – which was something he hadn't done before. 'That's where the challenge comes. And, of course, the reward.'

'Is this imposture and impersonation criminal?'

'Decidedly not. Morally, that's to say.'

'Morally?'

'Everybody concerned will be happier and better off than they would otherwise have been. So it just *can't* be wrong, can it?'

'But a judge might think it wrong? I might be put in quod?'

'Oh, most decidedly. You must be absolutely *clear* about that, my dear George, from the start. If you were found out, they'd put you away for years.'

'And you as well.'

'Certainly – if they could get hold of me.' Nicholas Comberford smiled cheerfully. 'The fact that we were in it together would make it conspiracy, or something like that. And they always make out that conspiracy is particularly bad. It just shows how unfair the law can be. Two chaps, and the penalty ought to be halved. Four chaps, and it ought to be quartered. You'd think the justice of that would be absolutely obvious, wouldn't you? But the minds of magistrates don't work that way. They're unreasonable people. One should have nothing to do with them.'

'What's the risk of having something to do with them in this affair?'

'Enormous, in a way.' Comberford's cheerfulness seemed to be increasing. 'That's to say, an outsider would see it as that. But just have faith in your own star – and, well, the risk's merely minimal. You have *faith* in your star, haven't you?'

'Don't be silly. I haven't got a star.'

'But of course you have!' Comberford leant across the table. 'Let me pour you another drop of brandy, and you'll acknowledge the truth of what I say. *In vino veritas*, you know.'

Seeing no cogency in this particular application of the tag, Gadberry declined the brandy. His cigar, he found, had gone out, and this gave him a moment to think.

'You keep on talking about an old girl,' he said. 'Who is she, and just how does she come in?'

'She's my great-aunt. My Great-aunt Prudence. Just the right name for a great-aunt, wouldn't you say? Have you any great-aunts of your own, by the way?'

'No, I haven't. I haven't any relatives at all.'

'That's all to the good. But a recently deceased great-aunt might have been an advantage. Give you the wavelength of the relationship, so to speak. Still, you'll soon pick it up. And it's not all you'll pick up.' Comberford paused to do himself a further generous tot of brandy. 'She's one of the wealthiest women in England.' He looked seriously at Gadberry. 'Yes,' he said. 'Let's face it. She's precisely that.'

5

'But lonely, too,' Comberford went on. 'Great-aunt Prudence is terribly lonely. That's why there's such a strong ethical slant to what we're fixing up. The great-nephew comes home, and comforts her declining years. It's a beautiful thought.'

'Wouldn't it be more beautiful if you did the job yourself, instead of trying to cheat this old woman in some way?' Gadberry was trying his truculent note again. 'If you have an elderly relative just rolling in money why the hell don't you weigh right in?'

'I'm a drunk, old boy.' Comberford tapped his brandy glass meaningfully. 'You must have noticed that by this time.'

'Perhaps I've had a glimmer of it.' It was true that Gadberry had been remarking to himself that Comberford was drinking a good deal more than seemed prudent in the course of a negotiation so tricky as the one he was attempting. 'But you could control it, couldn't you, if it was a matter of getting in on a fortune?'

'Not a hope. But *you* could, my dear George. Do you drink a lot?'

'Of course I drink a lot.'

'But, if you wanted to, you could stop drinking tomorrow?'

'I don't know. I've never thought. Yes, I'm pretty sure I could.'

'I'm glad to hear it. And it won't just be a matter of cutting down. You won't get a drop on the premises, and it will be as much as your life's worth to admit to getting a drop elsewhere. Aunt Prudence – we'll call her plain "Aunt" – is quite rabid. But I must be frank with you. That's only one reason why I can't turn up on her in my own dutiful and affectionate person. I live in the south of France, you see.

31

It turns more damnably expensive every year. There won't be any difficulty, I can tell you, in putting my share to good use.'

'Your share?'

'Don't worry. There's going to be plenty. Besides I'm a generous chap, as so many drunks are. Fifty-fifty's what I've decided on.'

'You mean you'll just go on living on the Riviera?'

'Oh, certainly. Under another name, of course. In fact, I do that for a greater part of the time already. It's quite easy. And Lulu doesn't mind.'

'Lulu?'

'She's another reason why I couldn't possibly go and live with the old girl. I couldn't possibly part with Lulu. Or not until her successor was absolutely in the bag. I'm a sensualist, old boy.'

'I see.' Gadberry, although he wouldn't have described himself as a notably moral young man, for some reason found this an absolutely revolting remark. 'If you've decided against your Aunt Prudence,' he said, 'your Aunt Prudence is damned lucky.'

'Oh, dear me, yes. Precisely. I'd break her heart, poor old soul, within a week. That's why it's lucky I'm now fixed up with a deputy.'

'Where does she live?' Gadberry asked – rather against his will. He realised that every question he put must have the effect of drawing him further in. He wanted to ask quite a number, all the same. Comberford's weird proposal was coming to exercise some sort of spell over him.

'The place is called Bruton Abbey. It's in one of the Yorkshire dales. A little remote, perhaps, for some tastes. Are you fond of country life?'

'No. At least, I don't suppose so. I've never tried it – or not to speak of.'

'Well, that's a trifle awkward.' For the first time, Comberford appeared a shade discouraged. 'You can't hunt, or fish, or shoot?'

'I wouldn't say that.' Gadberry's class-consciousness was stirred. 'I had an uncle who made me do these things, from time to time. They didn't interest me, but I expect I could still get by. At least with the patter. I might be a bit unpractised on the simple muscular side. Do

I understand, by the way, that your Aunt Prudence has a whole abbey to herself?'

'Certainly she has. And there's an enormous estate. Incidentally, it's a real abbey. It isn't even a seventeenth-century house quarried out of the ruins of one, which is the usual thing. It's an actual Cistercian monastery, in a very nice state of preservation.'

'Comfortable?'

'I haven't been there since I was a kid, when anything was luxurious compared with my expensive private school. You know?'

'I know.'

'Frankly, it's my guess that the *comfort moderne* will be on the patchy side. One always has to sacrifice snugness when in the pursuit of real style. Think of all those continental palaces. Of course, you'll be able to fix up your own quarters according to your own ideas. Aunt Prudence shows every sign of being extremely generous. Quirky, perhaps. Even demanding, in a way. But splendidly regardless in the matter of adding an extra nought at the end of a cheque. You see, George, how fair I'm being with you. The light and the shadow, so to speak. They're all going into the picture.'

'I just don't see any picture, so far.' Gadberry abandoned the stump of his cigar. He sat up straight. The moment had come, he saw, to see once and for all whether there was anything for him in this or not. 'What sort of age is your Aunt Prudence?'

'Oh, she's as old as the hills. Don't forget she's really a great-aunt. She can't last long.'

'You mean you want me to take on a life sentence?' It was with real astonishment that Gadberry produced this.

'Well, yes – but *her* life, my dear George. A spell of two or three years, at the most. As a matter of fact, poor old Aunt Prudence has some progressive and fatal heart disease. Only don't, by the way, mention it to her. She's said to be touchy about it.'

'I hang on until she dies, and after that there's money?'

'After that there's *big* money. Or rather, after that there's *astronomical* money. There will be big money straightaway. She's been absolutely

specific about it. It's in her letter. The bit about my – meaning your
– *menus frais.*'

'What's that?'

'The same as *menus plaisirs.* Pocket money on the scale appropriate
to an English gentleman. Haven't I shown you her letter?'

'Of course you haven't shown me her letter.'

'Well, here it is.' Comberford began to fish in his pockets. 'It's
yours for keeps, I need hardly say. Your letter of credence, so to speak.
Five thousand.'

'What do you mean – five thousand?'

'Pounds, George. Solid pounds sterling. And tax-free, mark you.
The old girl will just shell it out of her current income without
noticing.'

'That's not possible.' Gadberry felt it necessary to display himself
as a man of affairs. 'Nobody could part with £5,000 a year without
noticing. Not nowadays. Not with Surtax, and so forth.'

'My dear man, it will come out of capital appreciation, and all that.
These are regions that poor devils like you and me simply don't know
about. But £2,500 each will be something, you'll agree. Until the old
girl's funeral, that is. After that – Glory Hallelujah. Ah! Here it is.'

Comberford had produced a crumpled envelope, which he now
tossed across the table to Gadberry.

'Read, George,' he said. 'Read and admire.'

My dear Nicholas,

*It may surprise you to hear from me. It would certainly
surprise me to hear from you, since you have proved for many
Years an indifferent epistolary Correspondent. Indeed, I well recall
that when, in your Schooldays, I endeavoured to enter upon an
Exchange of Letters with a View to assisting in the settling of your
Principles and the forming of your Mind, your Replies to my
Observations and Reflections were so scanty as eventually to
make me abandon the Task.*

*I do not write, however, with any Idea of reprehending you in
this or any other Regard. Our last Meeting, as you will recall, was*

eight Years ago, upon the Occasion of your brief Visit to Bruton for the purpose of attending your Great-uncle Magnus' Funeral. I was much pleased by your Bearing upon that Occasion. It was religious without Ostentation and respectful without Servility. I found myself forming a good Opinion of your Parts...

George Gadberry interrupted his reading at this point for the purpose of giving his companion a surprised stare.

'The old lady was *pleased*?' he said. 'Pleased with *you*? And thought you quite a chap? Have you changed a lot?'

'Not in the least.' Comberford was unoffended by these questions. 'I simply put my best foot forward. I thought something might come of it. But nothing did – at the time. I suppose Aunt Prudence thought I was too old to tip. Now read on.'

'Isn't her style a bit odd? All those capital letters and long words. It's almost Victorian.'

'Nothing of the sort, George. It's Augustan. I suppose she was brought up on the essays of Joseph Addison, and stuff of that sort.'

'She's cracked, is she?'

'Well, not to any purpose. Not so that we could get her certified, or anything of that sort. But she does seem to take an occasional rum dip into the past. Mind you, I don't know much about her. I used to be at Bruton a lot as a kid, because I got on rather well with old Great-uncle Magnus. But I doubt whether I ever went back there after I was about fourteen. Except, as she says, for the old boy's funeral. I thought there might at least be a legacy. But he'd left every damned thing to his widow. Not that he had all that to leave. Old Magnus' father had been the younger son of a marquis, so he was the Hon., and all that. But he wasn't much in the way of the lovely Mun. Prudence, on the other hand, was a great heiress.'

'And is she the Hon., too?'

'Oh, certainly. Her father was some sort of political character who was made a peer. I remember it made addressing thank-you letters to them at Christmas rather tricky. I think it was "The Hon. Magnus

Minton and the Hon. Mrs Minton". It wasn't possible to get it shorter.'

'What awful rot!' Gadberry said. He was impressed. 'Your great-aunt's name is Minton?'

'Yes. Her maiden name, of course, was Comberford.'

'If I go into this, am I an Hon., too?'

'If you mean do I myself possess a title of honour, I don't.' Comberford smiled cheerfully. 'Although I'm bound to say I've found it useful to assume one from time to time.'

'I suppose you're what's called an adventurer. But I'm blessed if I see why I should do your adventuring for you. Or that the thing's remotely feasible.'

'Read on, my dear chap, read on.'

6

...I found myself forming a good Opinion of your Parts, even while judging them in large Measure regrettably unimproved by Habits of Study and Application: this although I was greatly pleased by what you communicated to me of your Efforts on behalf of the dumb Creation. The Practice in Question is assuredly not less reprehensible than that allied continental Abomination, the Devouring of Horses!

Gadberry broke off a second time.

'What on earth is that about?' he demanded.

'For goodness sake don't keep on interrupting. It was simply that I happened to be living in rather a pleasant part of Italy at the time, and Aunt Prudence wanted to know why. I couldn't say that it was because of the climate, and the inexpensive wine, and a girl, and so on. So I said I was organising a crusade against turning donkeys into cold sausages. You know the stuff. It's called *mortadella*.'

'There you are! I told you your whole plan is crazy.' Gadberry tossed Mrs Minton's letter contemptuously on the table. 'On the very first evening, at dinner and over our second glass of barley-water, she'd say "How about the *mortadella*?" Or she'd say that in whatever way Addison would have said it. And I'd merely goggle at her. Can't you see?'

'There are difficulties, of course.' Comberford's assurance appeared unruffled. 'But there are ways round them, as well. You'll come on one way round them when you turn over the page. So carry on.'

'Oh, very well.' With some reluctance, Gadberry retrieved the letter and resumed his reading.

I was the more gratified in that, as a Boy, you had been not without a censurable Predisposition to take Satisfaction in the Tormenting of the humblest Creatures. There was the Episode of the Belgian Hare; there was the yet more deplorable Episode of the faithful Tiger.

'For pity's sake!' This time Gadberry threw up his arms in despair. 'Can't you see, you fool? What sort of figure should I cut in the course of a little reminiscent chat about the faithful tiger? And who ever heard of a faithful tiger, anyway?'

'My dear chap, Tiger was an Aberdeen terrier. And you're coming, quite precisely, to the crunch. Just try the next paragraph.'

It is true that, in your Great-uncle's copious Memoirs, these Incidents were balanced, perhaps outweighed, by numerous Recollections of the less unendearing Traits of your Childhood. It was only a few Days after his Funeral, indeed, that, having your Future much upon my Mind, I thought to refresh my Memory by consulting those valuable Papers. Alas, upon going to the Cupboard in the Library in which I knew them to have long reposed, I made the sad Discovery that they were no longer extant. Such was the noble Modesty of your Great-uncle's Nature that he had undoubtedly destroyed the entire Series of his interesting Memorabilia *shortly before his Demise.*

'You see?' It was Comberford who interrupted this time, and he did so in a tone of triumph. 'The old dotard had scribbled copiously for years on every trivial event of his life. And I carried off the lot.'

'You *what*?'

'The day after the funeral. I was inspired, you see. It can only be called that. The thought simply came to me that the stuff might be useful one day. So I nipped into the library and collected it. There's nothing, absolutely nothing, in the old girl's memories of my visits to Bruton as a kid that isn't more than matched in the old boy's scribblings. Just read the rubbish through, and you can cap every recollection that Aunt Prudence has with half a dozen more. As for what happened in the couple of days I was there for the funeral, I can give you that *verbatim*. The thing's foolproof, George. It would be foolproof even if you *were* a fool – which you're not.'

Gadberry stared at Comberford with a kind of fascinated horror. For the first time, the fantastic proposal he was up against seemed to him to have veered into the region of the possible.

'Look here!' he said wildly, 'let's get back to essentials. People just *can't* successfully impersonate each other. The mere physical thing's unworkable. Are we really all that like each other? I don't believe it. And our mannerisms and intonations and so forth are totally different. The deception would blow up in the first ten minutes.'

'It would blow up then – *or never. Le premier pas,* as I said before. And we are extravagantly like each other – far more than I could reasonably have hoped. Or rather, you're extravagantly like me five or six years ago.'

'There you are, then. This isn't five or six years ago. It's –'

'Don't be an ass, George. It's precisely the point that will make your acceptance instantaneous – not only by Aunt Prudence, but by any remaining servants who were around at the time of the funeral. That's psychology, old chap.'

'But think of things like passports, bank accounts, signatures, proofs of –'

'Poppycock. Aunt Prudence will simply march you in on her bank manager, and you'll find the fellow has put down the red carpet. And so with the family solicitor and everybody else. You just don't realise the enormous respectability of the position you are going to enjoy. For instance, when you go into the village church on Sunday to read the Lessons –'

'When I *what*?'

'Lord, yes. You'll have to accept your responsibilities, you know. I don't disguise the fact from you for a moment. But, as I was saying, when you do that, do you expect the dear old vicar to step forward and demand documentary evidence that you are indeed the long-absent Nicholas Comberford? Of course not! Now, get on with Aunt

Prudence's letter. You haven't yet got to her proposal. And it's worth getting to.'

However, my own Recollection is very clear as to the high Regard in which my dear Husband held you in those early and formative Years. It was his Habit to remark that had you been born directly into the Line of our Properties, you would have come to justify the Privilege by an exact Attention to the Duties of such a Station.

At this point, Gadberry produced sharp laughter.

'Think of that!' he said. 'Your great-uncle, if you ask me, can't have had all that much stuffed between his ears.'

'I rather agree, George. But now, you'll find, the thing's coming. You're on the brink.'

These are, as you must be aware, difficult Times for the Landed interest. The Administration is unsympathetic, and make little Doubt but that the present Prime Minister – whose Name escapes me for the Moment – would be hard put to it to distinguish Wheat from Oats, or a Dog Fox from a Vixen. In such iron Times a strong Hand is needed for the management of large Estates, and although much may reasonably be left to one's Agents, Bailiffs and Men of Business it is nevertheless increasingly incumbent upon one to exercise a strict Surveillance...

Once more, Gadberry broke off abruptly.

'I ask you!' he said. 'How the hell am I going to manage an estate? The notion's absurd.'

'That's all rot. It's simply that the old girl is failing –'

'Her letter doesn't read as if she's failing.'

'Well, she is. Only a year or two to go, as I've said. And she's beginning to fuss. Of course those agents and bailiffs and people are perfectly competent to do their job. They wouldn't thank you for really trying to poke your nose in. You'll just ride around now and then to have an affable word with the tenants. Nothing more than that. And now, George, go on to what the old girl's prepared to run to.'

It is this, my dear Nicholas, that I have determined to call upon you to do. Although hale of Body and – I believe – of Mind, I am yet conscious that my Years require me to give serious Thought no less to Matters temporal than to Matters eternal. If I am to discharge the Duties of the Station to which it has pleased Providence to call me, I must give anxious Consideration to the Future of Bruton – and that alike in the Choice of its Proprietor and the Well-being and proper Control of its labouring Poor. Are you likely to be a just Repository of my Confidence in these Regards? It is in an Endeavour to determine this all-important Issue that I now make the following probationary Proposal.

First, you shall present yourself to me at Bruton with all convenient Speed. Secondly, being domesticated here, you shall with all due Diligence endeavour to prove yourself worthy of my Trust. Thirdly, and in return, I shall make you an annual Allowance of Money – an Allowance which must be neither improperly lavish nor, on the other hand, improperly exiguous in the Light of our Consequence in the County. Five thousand Pounds suggests itself to me as a reasonable Figure. And fourthly, when your Competence and Probity shall have declared themselves to my Satisfaction, I will execute the requisite Instruments for establishing you as my sole Heir.

Gadberry stopped reading, and for some moments kept silence. When at length he did speak, it appeared to be out of a sort of desperation.

'But I *couldn't!*' he cried. 'It's inconceivable.'

'What's inconceivable?'

'Living, in this awful abbey-place, with an old woman who talks like that.'

'Perhaps she doesn't talk quite as she writes. It's a very formal letter, after all.'

'Her proposal's utter bosh. There's no sense in it.'

'On the contrary, it's thoroughly businesslike. You turn up at Bruton on probation, as she says, and make do for a year on the £5,000. In fact it looks as if you – which means you and I, old chap – go on making do on that modest allowance even when she's proceeded with what she calls her requisite instruments and has appointed you as her heir. Her doing *that* is the crucial point. She must be persuaded to sign on the dotted line pretty soon. It must be done before there's any suspicion of her going gaga and incompetent. On the other hand, it would be hazardous to force the pace. You'll have to use your discretion.'

'She'll have to make a new will?'

'Oh, decidedly.'

'Isn't it an odd way to dispose of a great estate – leaving the bequeathing of it to so late a date? It just asks for enormous death duties, and so on.'

'Perfectly true, George. I see that you already possess a very useful sense of these things. And it's a pity, I agree. Still, there will be plenty to divide up, all the same. Now, just skim through the rest of the thing to yourself. And I'll go and look up a train.'

'You'll do *what*?' It was with difficulty that George Gadberry articulated this question. He was feeling suddenly breathless and a little sick.

'Lord, yes. The plunge is the thing. Put it off for a week, and you'd simply funk it. Candidly, I'd do just that myself. But don't give yourself time to think, and all will be well.'

'What about those memoirs, or whatever they are, by your Great-uncle Magnus?' Gadberry found himself clutching at this as at a straw. 'Oughtn't I to give myself a week or two to get them up?'

'Good Lord, no! Incidentally, I've got them with me in one of my suitcases, and they're yours from this moment. Just read through the first hundred pages or so on your way down, and start talking on the strength of them at once. You can imagine the sort of thing. "Do you remember, Aunt Prudence, how angry you were when I helped the red-haired stable boy to drown the kittens?" There will be lots of that sort. Maintain a pious and dutiful attitude towards the memory of old Magnus, and you'll have her eating out of your hand.'

Comberford drained the last drop of brandy in his glass, prudently pushed away the bottle, and got to his feet.

'*Nicholas*, old boy,' he said, 'good luck!'

PART TWO

SOME PROBLEMS OF A COUNTRY GENTLEMAN

7

George Gadberry (as he had formerly been) climbed out of his bath. He remembered to do so with due care, so that this time he succeeded in not overturning it. It was that sort of bath – like a child's portable paddling-pool, but with a sloping back at one end against which it was just possible to recline in a gingerly way for purposes of maximum luxury. It was, in fact, a hip-bath. Not many minutes ago, it had been filled, hot-water jug by hot-water jug, by two housemaids. Presently, when George had signified his vacating his dressing-room by ringing a bell, these handmaidens would return and empty it – just how, he had not yet discovered – before shoving it away in a cupboard. If the bath itself was not particularly enjoyable, these ancillary circumstances somehow were. There was something almost Homeric in being thus tended. George had made, indeed, no improper advances to these young persons, since he was still so eminently in the position of feeling that he just couldn't be too careful. But he did beguile this dressing hour with a little harmless fantasy, vaguely feudal in suggestion. The younger of his two attendants was not ill-favoured. And he was a kind of lord of the manor, after all.

George whistled as he dried himself – and did so with a cheerfulness not much diminished by the knowledge that he would never in actual fact get very far as a routine seducer of innocence. The excitements of love tended to assail him romantically, intermittently, and upon occasion catastrophically, rather than in a steady and businesslike fashion. Going after these maidens, he suspected, would turn out to be rather a shabby role, carrying an uncomfortable suggestion of a lack of fair play. Reflecting thus, he tossed away his enormous towel, stopped whistling, and frowned instead. These streaks of fastidiousness puzzled him. They certainly didn't seem to go with his present enterprise, which could only be described as vastly unscrupulous. For he was now well launched on a criminal imposture. And the really odd thing was that he appeared – intermittently at least – to be enjoying it.

A clean white shirt had been laid out on a chair, with a cuff link already inserted in one side of each cuff. He donned this and buttoned it up. He tied his black tie. Silk socks, dress trousers, pumps: on they all went. Such a ritual, followed seven nights a week, ought to have been extremely boring, but he had to confess to himself that so far he had found it quite fun. It wasn't, indeed, entirely unvaried. On Sundays – and this was a Sunday – Aunt Prudence liked him to don the red velvet smoking jacket. He put it on now, and admired its silk facings in his looking-glass. Conceivably such things were no longer made. This one had belonged to Uncle Magnus, but it fitted him very well. He was pleasantly aware of something symbolical in his being enjoined to wear it. It was a sort of token that his acceptance at Bruton was already assured.

Gadberry glanced at his watch, and saw that he had fifteen minutes to spare before going downstairs. So he had better put in a little time with the *Memoirs*. He still kept these locked in a suitcase, and when he consulted them it was always with an ear cocked for anybody approaching his room. The housemaids would make nothing of them, but it would be different with the butler, Boulter, or with Aunt Prudence's companion, Miss Bostock. Miss Bostock, indeed, he had come to regard as the danger-point in his whole enterprise, for she was a well-established inmate of the Abbey whom Nicholas Comberford had failed to mention.

Fortunately it was difficult to be surprised unawares in a building that went in so massively for stone-flagged and uncarpeted corridors. Only a ghost could bring off anything of the sort. There were several ghosts, it seemed, at Bruton Abbey. But none of them had put in an appearance yet. Perhaps their activities took place on a seasonal basis, as with so much else in this part of the world. If the affair really went on indefinitely – Gadberry thought – nothing was going to take more getting used to than the importance the calendar assumes in a rural environment. If you had grown up to regard winter simply as so many months in which you have to put shillings rather more frequently into the gas meter, or summer as indicating nothing more than a changed weight of underwear, then you found it quite a business to get on terms with the fact that the earth's annual wobble on its axis (or whatever it was) really has significance for the life of man. It was having that now. Winter had arrived. The Abbey was very cold.

Gadberry got out a volume of the *Memoirs* and went into his office. This was the name he had decided to give to his comfortably appointed, if not very adequately heated, sitting-room. For country gentlemen, it had appeared, always have offices. They keep accounts and things in a safe there. They interview tenants and give them whisky. If the place is very grand (and Bruton *was* very grand) they hold conferences with a perfect gentleman known as the Agent. Gadberry held such conferences with Mrs Minton's Agent, a person of vaguely military provenance called Captain Fortescue. Fortescue and he had arrived, Gadberry felt, at a very good understanding. Major matters were settled Fortescue's way, but with a great air of having been thought up by Gadberry. Minor matters were also settled Fortescue's way, but this time with Fortescue being given high marks for vigilance and efficiency. It was a discreet and civilised arrangement, reflecting, Gadberry thought, credit on both of them. Certainly it kept Great-aunt Prudence happy, and this was clearly something laudable in itself. The old girl was a benefactor. It was their business to do her proud.

Not – Gadberry reminded himself, as he settled down for a few minutes relaxation – that he and Fortescue were remotely in a conspiracy. Fortescue was entirely honest, and therefore potentially an enemy. *All* honest men were that. The thought was a little daunting. It made Gadberry feel lonely.

He reached for a decanter, and poured himself a glass of sherry. The decanter was a beautiful affair of Waterford glass, and it had been given him by Aunt Prudence. There was a puzzle in this – a puzzle that had several times made him feel distinctly uneasy. Aunt Prudence was certainly not given to swimming in alk, and she appeared never to have heard of cocktails. But wine was served, if sparingly, at meals, and the old girl appeared to have no feelings whatever about one's private habits in this regard. How could Comberford – the real Nicholas Comberford – have been so ill-informed in the matter? It was actually her fanatical objection to liquor that he had advanced as a principal reason for his inability to face the prospect of domestication at Bruton Abbey himself. Perhaps Aunt Prudence had entirely changed her views over the past few years. But Gadberry had gathered no hint to support this hypothesis, and the little fishing for information which he had ventured upon with Boulter had yielded at least a presumption the other way.

As Gadberry sipped his sherry now, this small mystery seemed suddenly to assume a sinister significance – as indeed it had done before. He'd have liked to be able to ask Comberford how he had got the thing wrong. But this wasn't possible, if only because he had no idea where Comberford was. The man had given him no address. He'd made no suggestion of any actual means whereby he might receive his half of the £5,000 a year as it came in; he'd merely murmured that all this would settle itself later. Presumably he had returned to Lulu and his Riviera leisure, and would communicate with Gadberry when he wanted to. But surely this was a crazy state of affairs? Surely, in the event of some unforeseen crisis, Gadberry ought to be able to get hold of the real Comberford at once? Yet it just couldn't be done. There was no line through Mr Norval Falsetto and his agency. The Chester Court had known only Mr John Smith of the beard and the dark glasses. The second hotel Gadberry had not so much as noticed the name of, and he much doubted whether he could find his way to it if he wanted to. There were scores of such establishments in that part of London.

Not for the first time, Gadberry found himself wondering about the competence of Nicholas Comberford. Had he fixed up this whole imposture on a hopelessly amateur and ramshackle basis? Or was there something rather deep about him? These were disturbing questions, and no doubt it would be best to push them out of mind now and give this final fifteen minutes before dinner to a few pages of the *Memoirs*, as planned.

Gadberry opened the volume he had selected. It dealt with the first summer during which, upon his annual holiday at Bruton, the young Nicholas Comberford had been promoted to his own pony. This was as far back in the *Memoirs* as Gadberry had researched so far, and it was proving to be rich in valuable anecdotal matter. But Nicholas had been no more than five. How much about one's five-year-old self does one remember? Gadberry found that he had to review his own authentic childhood in order to get a measure of what might be plausible in the case of his spurious one, and that this process of comparison was not without its dangers. It would never do to try feeding Aunt Prudence with reminiscences actually drawn from Gadberry and not Comberford family history.

Aunt Prudence… Was it a little odd that he had really come to think of Mrs Minton as that? Gadberry closed the *Memoirs*. They just weren't holding his attention. For here was another field of speculation which produced uneasy feelings. Of course it was very convenient that he had fallen so easily into his part. Every now and then, and with alarming unexpectedness, danger did appear. It wasn't in the nature of the case that Bruton shouldn't, so to speak, pack dynamite in its every mouldering corner. He might be betrayed, suddenly and irrevocably, in a hundred different ways. Yet his moments of actual panic had been few, and were becoming fewer. He was ceasing to believe that he could be exposed. But why was he ceasing to believe it? *Why?*

Gadberry finished his sherry, glanced again at his watch, and for the first time gave himself a straight answer. It was because, all unconsciously, he was ceasing to believe that the imposture *was* an imposture. To put the matter very moderately, he was ceasing wholly and simply to believe that he was George Gadberry. There was an increasing component in him – one had to use some such word as that – which was quite willing to *be* Nicholas Comberford. It was this component that said, and thought, 'Aunt Prudence' so spontaneously.

A lay imposter (so to speak) might have judged this all to the good. But Gadberry, being a professional actor, understood the hazard it presented. Cease to be conscious of your part *as* a part, and in no time you will be playing it damned badly. He had been relying on his professional approach to safeguard him from what he had somewhere read about as the chief risk which imposters run. It was just this risk of losing grip on the fact that one *was* an imposter. As with actors, in fact, so with this particular form of criminal. Lose the sense of artifice, and the role dies on you. You may even come to believe that you really are what you set out to pretend to be. In other words, the job of being an imposter round the clock can play queer tricks with you, and finally send you off your rocker. Gadberry seemed to remember reading in a history book at school that Perkin Warbeck, or perhaps it was Lambert Simnel, had really believed himself to be one of the Princes in the Tower.

This was all very uncomfortable. Gadberry had no fancy for finding himself edged into something like a play by Pirandello. Gadberry pretending to be Comberford, however legally reprehensible, was rather fun. Gadberry believing himself to be Comberford was quite a different matter.

Of course all these fancies were merely morbid. There was no risk of anything of the sort really happening. Only he did find himself wishing he was in contact with just *one* person who *knew* he was Gadberry. It would even be a comfort to feel there was at least one person who *suspected* he was not really –

Gadberry pulled himself up abruptly. That way, surely, madness did veritably lie. But the thought had brought the true Comberford back into his head. Comberford was the only person in the world who knew who he – George Gadberry, living here at Bruton Abbey – authentically was. Gadberry found himself wishing that, every now and then, he could conduct a secret nocturnal telephone conversation with Comberford – this on the pretext of reporting progress, seeking advice.

What if he never saw, or heard of, Comberford again?

This extraordinary question sprang up in Gadberry's mind just as he was getting to his feet for the purpose of making his way to Mrs Minton's drawing-room. It seemed entirely senseless – but there it was. Suppose that Comberford had been acting in furtherance of some plot quite other than his declared one, and that this entailed his vanishing for ever? And suppose Comberford's existence – as an entity, so to speak, distinct from George Gadberry – was unprovable? Suppose this to be so, and that Gadberry himself for some reason wanted to *stop* being Comberford? Suppose his conscience troubled him, so that he tried to *confess*? Would he be believed? Or would it just be taken for granted that poor Nicholas Comberford had gone mad, and had better be shut up in an asylum where he could scream his head off to the effect that he was really somebody called Gadberry?

Needless to say, Gadberry hadn't taken ten paces down the corridor before he was able to assure himself that all this was utter nonsense, and that now he had better pull himself together. If he wanted to go not to an asylum, but to jail tomorrow in his own authentic character there was certainly nothing to stop him. He had only to ring up the local police and tell them the truth. But, of course, he wanted to do nothing of the sort. He was – he assured himself – enjoying the whole thing, and it was only the very fact of his pursuing his imposture so successfully that had perversely started these bizarre ideas in his head. Still, he saw that they were ideas which had, so to speak, a psychological basis. He had been so readily taken for Nicholas Comberford, the mantle was now so securely enfolding him, that he was in danger of succumbing to some primitive and irrational sense that he was being deprived of his own identity. There was insecurity in the very fact of his having – in another sense – achieved security so easily. Yes, that was it. A little steadied by this piece of self-analysis, Gadberry made his way to his dinner.

8

There had been a certain exaggeration in Comberford's statement that Bruton Abbey was a Cistercian monastery in a very nice state of preservation. It was true, however, that it incorporated substantial parts of the actual fabric of such a place, and that this had certain curious architectural consequences. Gadberry's quarters, having been in fact the Abbot's lodging, were connected with the main building only by a long corridor of excessive gloom. Off this there opened on one side a series of cells. And they really were cells. Recalcitrant monks had been accommodated in them – presumably so that they could be suitably disciplined at any time under the personal supervision of their superior. The whole place, Gadberry thought, must have been like a nightmarish sort of public school. That was certainly why nineteenth-century Mintons had preserved it so carefully; it was an ideal setting for the virtuous discomfort which that era judged good for the soul. There was, no doubt, a certain amusement in having a drawing-room in which the stone benches of the original chapter house were still incorporated – as there was, too, in keeping guns and fishing rods in a particularly chilly calefactory. But what used to be called the Gothic Taste had surely had its day. If he ever really had to take Bruton in hand – which of course he wouldn't have to do – he would begin operations by simply knocking it down. If, that was to say, it *could* be knocked down. For the whole place seemed as massive as the British Museum or St Paul's Cathedral.

Boulter was lurking in the murkily glassed-in cloister. He considered it part of his duties to apprise Gadberry of any company to be encountered in the drawing-room.

'Good evening, sir,' he said. 'You will find that the old Sunday custom obtains.'

This was a new one; Gadberry hadn't heard it before. Nevertheless the *Memoirs* enabled him to get on top of it in a moment.

'Ah, yes,' he replied easily. 'The locals, eh?'

'Precisely, sir. It was Mr Minton's habit to set aside Sunday evenings for local society. The County would be entertained during the week.'

'We don't do much of that nowadays, do we?'

'No, sir. I am afraid it must be a little quiet for you. Mrs Minton no longer feels an obligation to move much in her own circles. But there is an obligation, of course, in regard to the local people.'

'The vicar, I suppose?'

'Yes, sir – Mr Grimble. And Dr and Mrs Pollock.'

'Well, that's very pleasant.' Gadberry moved towards the drawing-room door with an expression of mild good cheer. He didn't in fact expect much entertainment from the society of either an elderly clergyman or an elderly sawbones and his wife. But unruffled good humour was his line at Bruton. Besides, such occasions did have what he supposed was a certain period charm.

He entered the drawing-room, said the right thing to Aunt Prudence, went round shaking hands with the three guests, and then said the right things to Miss Bostock. Miss Bostock, being only a superior employee, came last – but, by the same token, had to be accorded particular courtesy. Some minutes of suitably constrained general conversation followed. And then Boulter announced that dinner was served.

The dining-room at Bruton had been the refectory of the *conversi* or lay brethren. Although no longer three hundred feet long (much of it had disappeared) it would still have afforded a reasonably spacious setting for a City banquet. The six people now sitting down, therefore, would have presented to a dispassionate eye something of the effect of a small scurry of mice in a cathedral. It wasn't warm; it wasn't, in fact, other than exceedingly cold; but as snow was beginning to fall outside, this wasn't altogether surprising. Gadberry found himself speculating a little apprehensively as to what the Abbey would be like when winter – a robust Yorkshire winter – really set in.

Mrs Minton had motioned Dr Pollock to the place on her right, so Gadberry did the same by the doctor's wife. That meant having Miss Bostock on his left. She could do most of her talking with Pollock, Gadberry decided, and that would leave Mrs Pollock for him. The Pollocks were very low down on his danger list; although fairly long-established in the district, they hadn't been around back in the days when the young Nicholas Comberford used to visit Bruton. Grimble was another matter. The tenth son, or thereabout, of some deceased Yorkshire bigwig, he had held the living of Bruton since the first day it had been at all decent to induct him into it. Fortunately that was incredibly long ago, and Grimble was so far sunk in senile confusion that people seldom attended to what he said.

'Mr Grimble,' Mrs Minton was saying in what Gadberry thought of as her grand manner, 'will you please say – '

'*Benedictus benedicat.*' Grimble, who had a beard like an untidy bird's nest, tumbled out the words, slumped into his chair, and grasped his soup spoon in a trembling hand. Nobody was surprised by this unbecoming conduct, since all had observed it in him before. Perhaps, Gadberry thought, he was systematically deprived of adequate nourishment by an unscrupulous housekeeper. More probably he was merely reverting to the first and uncorrected manners of his nursery. But now, not yet having been provided with anything upon which to begin blunting his appetite, Grimble was glancing impatiently up and down the table. His gaze fell on Gadberry – and stayed there.

'Young man,' Grimble said, 'who are you? Who are you, I say?'

Nobody attended to this except Gadberry. He told himself instantly that it meant nothing at all, but this didn't prevent his feeling a nasty shock, all the same. For one thing, although it was polite for the others to appear not to have heard, it was polite in him to make a friendly and unperturbed reply. 'I'm Nicholas,' he ought to explain. Or (remembering the *Memoirs*) perhaps he ought to expand to 'I'm Nicholas, who brought the white mice into Sunday school'. Or would that be the wrong note? Would it be more courteous to concur (so to speak) in the assumption that something like a formal introduction was needed, and say with a bow 'I am Mrs Minton's great-nephew, sir. My name is Nicholas Comberford'?

'Fellow hasn't a tongue in his head.'

Gadberry realised that when he ought to have been saying something he had been thinking what to say. It didn't, of course, really matter in this instance, but it did represent his breaking a rule. It was always better to trust to the spur of the moment than to give any appearance of a pause for calculation.

'He has a look of young Nicholas, you know, of young Nicholas.' Grimble had turned to his hostess and, between gulps of soup, offered this informatively. 'Only young Nicholas would always speak up. Well do I remember the occasion upon which I caught him stealing my strawberries. He was under the net, you know, under the net. So he couldn't get away. And I was carrying a switch, I was carrying a switch, I say.' Grimble produced a high-pitched cackle of laughter, and then slid more soup with surprising dexterity through a slit in the bird's nest. 'So he spoke up, you know, he spoke up loudly.'

'Mr Grimble's memory isn't quite right.' Gadberry addressed the table at large, and to the accompaniment of his sunniest smile. 'It was the coachman's boy who was under the net. I was astride the wall, with my strawberries already picked. And I was treacherously cheering on the vicar at his good work.'

'That is certainly correct.' Mrs Minton nodded her head emphatically. 'My dear husband made a note of it at the time. A Comberford, he justly remarked, would not readily let himself be caught in the net.' Mrs Minton looked down the table. Although the story didn't really appear to represent her great-nephew in a wholly amiable light, she took evident satisfaction in it. Indeed, she expatiated on this now. 'I am glad, my dear Nicholas, that you hold so much of that early period in your memory. It is a very proper sort of piety. Boulter, we will take wine.'

The company took wine – and with reasonable elegance at this stage of the meal, since Boulter was instantly able to produce a suitable Madeira. Had Mrs Minton (as she was quite capable of doing) not uttered these words until her guests had munched their way to the other end of the feast, Boulter would have been equally dextrous in the production of Sauterne. Gadberry had a high regard for Boulter's professional accomplishment. When he became master of Bruton – he found himself thinking – he would probably keep Boulter on.

'One branch of the Comberfords, indeed,' Mrs Minton was proceeding, 'have a motto that is apposite here. It is *Cave Retiola*. Just what is meant by the little nets is obscure. But, in general, wariness is being enjoined. The injunction is at least a politic one.'

Gadberry agreed. To be wary of the little nets, he reflected, was precisely his business.

'I speak only of a cadet branch of my family. The motto of our own line, Nicholas, you know very well.'

This was awkward, and there was a slight pause. It was a piece of homework that Gadberry ought to have done long ago. Only he hadn't. That armigerous families have mottoes, coats of arms and the like just hadn't occurred to him.

'Hold everything!'

It was Dr Pollock who had enunciated this loudly and emphatically, so that for a moment Gadberry had a confused impression that the company was being summoned to confront some sudden crisis. But Mrs Minton was again nodding approvingly.

'Precisely,' she said. 'It is an excellent motto, and particularly to be regarded in the present age of legalised expropriation and robbery. One ought to give nothing away. Except, of course, in moderation, and to the good poor. At Bruton, however, it is very doubtful whether we any longer *have* good poor. People are either not poor, or not good. So the question does not arise. Nicholas, pray mark this.'

Gadberry did his best to look like one who marks this. In point of fact, he wasn't at all sure that he would much care to live up to this particular family motto. If he came into enormous wealth – enormous wealth even after the real Nicholas Comberford had received his whack – he would probably find it rather fun to give away quite a lot of money in various odd ways. The Bruton fortune was already coming to strike him as oppressive. Perhaps it was some sense of this that had motivated the real Nicholas to initiate his extraordinary deception; he wanted money without the feeling of being bludgeoned by it.

There was something alarming, Gadberry told himself, in his own intermittent tendency to go motive-hunting in this way on the real Nicholas' behalf; it touched off in him an obscure sense that the play in which he had been given so prominent a role was one that he didn't really have the hang of. But that way panic lay, and to avoid it he plunged abruptly into conversation with Miss Bostock on his left. In any case it was time that he had put up a little civil conversation to Aunt Prudence's companion.

'What do you think?' he asked. 'Would you agree that we have no good poor on the landscape?'

'I regard myself as most definitely in that category. I have no fortune. A settled amiability is my sole balance in the bank, and sometimes I feel I shall overdraw on it.' Miss Bostock, who went in for this astringent note in her conversation with Gadberry, gave him a steady look. 'Perhaps you have some fellow feeling for me in this?'

'I don't know that I have much amiability,' Gadberry said. 'But what I have I don't feel any drain upon. It's been wonderful coming back to Bruton, you know. I have always loved it.' He had decided long ago that ingenuousness of this sort was the safest line with Miss Bostock. 'Particularly in winter,' he added rather at random.

'You surprise me. It has been my impression that when you ceased to be of an age to be despatched here involuntarily your visits became infrequent. Is that inaccurate?'

'No, I think you are quite right.' Gadberry inwardly cursed the woman. She was coming to trail her coat quite a lot in this fashion.

She realised, no doubt, that there wasn't much future for her at Bruton now. 'Young men are often shockingly undutiful. And, of course, I had all sorts of irons in the fire.'

'You still have one or two, I imagine.'

Gadberry made no reply. He simply smiled, as if Miss Bostock's last remark had been a particularly pleasant one. In fact she was clearly telling him that she judged him to be a schemer and a parasite. And this, when one thought of it, was odd. It was true in a way. But it wasn't a truth that Miss Bostock could have any real glimmer of.

At least he could, for the moment, stop talking to the woman. So he turned to Mrs Pollock on his right, and prepared to say something to her. But Mrs Pollock, as it happened, spoke to him first.

'Mr Comberford,' Mrs Pollock asked, 'do you often see the Master now?'

9

Gadberry was so taken aback by this question that for a moment he supposed Mrs Pollock to have addressed him under the influence of religious enthusiasm, and to be directing her curiosity upon the privacies of his devotional life. Then he realised that this wasn't the state of the case at all; that the conversation had remained decently secular; and that the person thus alarmingly imported into it simply enjoyed, for one reason or another, the right to the designation Mrs Pollock had applied to him. And Gadberry's alarm had two occasions. He had been addressed during a lull in the not particularly lively talk that Mrs Minton's dinner-table produced, so that attention was now focused on him and everybody appeared to await his answer. And he *had* no answer. He had only – but this was something – a rapidly achieved grasp of what the problem was.

The Pollocks, he had told himself, were not dangerous. Their memories of Bruton didn't go back far enough. They had never set eyes on him until a few weeks ago. But in forming this opinion, he now saw, he had simply missed out, so to speak, a whole dimension of possibilities. Nicholas Comberford had scarcely been at Bruton since he was a boy. But he had, after all, been elsewhere. In one place or another, and named with his own name, he had lived in some sort of normal contact with his fellows. For a good many years, indeed, his residence seemed to have been mainly abroad. But there was always a possibility of running up against people who had known him, or at least against people who could dredge up some common acquaintance. This was almost certainly what was happening now.

But who was the Master? There was quite a range of possibilities. He might be an MFH. But Aunt Prudence had turned out not to approve of hunting, and was on somewhat chilly terms with its supporters in the neighbourhood. This reference, therefore, was unlikely. The heir apparent to a Scottish peerage, Gadberry knew, is frequently designated as the Master of This or That. Since Mintons and Comberfords were alike supposed to be persons of aristocratic pretention perhaps this was the territory involved. Mrs Pollock might for some reason know, for instance, that Nicholas Comberford had been at school with a Master in this sense, and be proposing to strike an agreeable social note with the topic. But then again, the thought of schools introduced another possibility. Some public schools – Wellington, for example – call their Headmaster plain Master. So there was that possibility too. Again, the heads of certain Oxford and Cambridge colleges are styled Master. But the real Nicholas Comberford was not a university man, any more than the false one was. So that didn't seem to help. Meanwhile, the silence was (to Gadberry's sense) painfully prolonging itself.

'Well, no,' he said. 'You see, I've been living abroad a good deal.'

'But that, of course, is why I ask.' Mrs Pollock's tone expressed surprise. 'Naturally,' she added.

Gadberry experienced an unpleasant sensation down his spine. Mrs Pollock struck him as an obstinate and tactless woman; she would press on with a piece of senseless chit-chat even when it had become evident that something had gone wrong with it. And it was just through the chink of some such small and peripheral occasion as this, Gadberry knew, that the waters of disaster might first trickle and then swell to a sudden flood. What *was* the answer?

'Mr Comberford,' Miss Bostock said suddenly, 'tell Mrs Pollock about the donkeys.'

'The donkeys?' Gadberry was bewildered. For one thing, although Aunt Prudence's companion did, through long association, occasionally fall into something like her employer's manner of speech, she had spoken in an oddly abrupt and commanding fashion.

'Your mention of residence abroad has put it in my mind. Your struggle against the *mortadella* factory.'

'Yes, of course.' Seizing on this as upon a straw, Gadberry plunged into elaborate improvisation. Considering the degree of his perturbation, he was conscious of doing it rather well. He found it hard to believe that Miss Bostock had not performed a deliberate rescue operation. But why on earth should she do so? She had never suggested herself to him as one alert to obviate minor social embarrassments. Yet any other motive than this opened up possibilities too dire to contemplate. Desperately, Gadberry talked on. Every now and then he stole a glance at Mrs Pollock in the endeavour to decide whether she was simply biding her time, determined to bob up again with her enigma as soon as opportunity offered. Fortunately, however, everybody was now following his recital with close attention. The Reverend Mr Grimble (although a little preoccupied with removing fish bones from his beard) was producing intermittent cackling noises evidently designed to betoken appreciation. And Mrs Minton herself was listening with the approval which she was always prepared to bestow upon this episode during her great-nephew's otherwise censurable expatriation.

But Gadberry couldn't continue to hold forth indefinitely, and eventually he stopped.

'Mr Comberford,' Mrs Pollock asked, 'do you often see the Master now?'

This time no succour came from Miss Bostock, whose attention had been demanded by Grimble across the table. Various counsels of desperation flashed through Gadberry's mind. He might say 'Certainly not: don't I hate the man's guts?' or 'Don't you know he was drowned at sea?' or even 'Not since they put him inside'. But although such shock tactics might stupefy this hideous woman into silence for the moment they could only lead to trouble later on. In any case, Gadberry was preserved from such rashness by Mrs Pollock's husband, who suddenly addressed her with marital brusqueness from Miss Bostock's other hand.

'Penelope,' he said, 'you're talking nonsense. It wasn't Comberford that the Master said he knew. It was the young fellow who seems likely to inherit the Hartleys' place at Spatchett. You should be more careful' – and Dr Pollock gave Gadberry a sharp glance – 'not to get your hopeful heirs mixed.'

Gadberry, although he couldn't fail to feel that this was a loaded remark, gave Dr Pollock a very sunny smile indeed. This particular crisis had collapsed. Indeed, Mrs Pollock had collapsed. Perhaps there was some shocking solecism in muddling Bruton and Spatchett. Mrs Minton certainly seemed to think so, for what she had heard of this exchange appeared to be occasioning her some displeasure.

'Spatchett?' she said. 'Doctor, did I hear you mention Spatchett? The Hartleys, I fear, have a very imperfect sense of their position. There is a young cousin who is almost bound to inherit the estate, such as it is.'

'Quite right,' Pollock said. 'I was just mentioning him.'

'The family, I am sorry to say, permitted him to undertake the study of medicine. It was a most unsuitable thing.'

'Ah!' Pollock said. This time he gave Gadberry a glance in which there seemed to lurk a malicious amusement. 'Perhaps you are right. I see your point of view.'

'It must be apparent to anybody.' Mrs Minton seemed quite unconscious that she was developing this conversation with her own medical attendant on anything other than wholly courteous lines. 'The young man even went to pursue his studies in Dublin, a city in which I am told that there is virtually no good society left. His interest, I believe, was in obstetrics. One would suppose that skill in the delivery of infants, should such an accomplishment be desired, could be acquired without crossing the Irish Sea and taking up residence among rebels and Fenians.'

'Well, they have rather a good place for that sort of thing. The Rotunda. The Master of the Rotunda is a top man at the job. We know the late one quite well, and this young Hartley frequently speaks about him. But his health isn't good, and he has retired to the

South of France. Something of the sort has just been running in my wife's head.'

So that explained *that*, Gadberry told himself – and went to work with renewed appetite on a plate of roast turkey. He still didn't feel quite happy in his mind. The behaviour of Miss Bostock had been odd and required thinking about. But at least the Master wouldn't bother him again.

'Moreover,' Mrs Minton was saying, 'the young man is as yet unmarried. Nicholas, I think that is correct?'

'Yes, Aunt Prudence. Of course. It's something I just haven't got round to thinking of.' Gadberry's response was rather at random. 'But I suppose I must find a nice girl one day.'

'Don't be foolish, Nicholas. I refer to the Hartley's heir, and to another instance of their negligence. It appears that they have taken no steps to secure an advantageous connection for the young man. Nothing could be more injudicious. He may suppose himself free to walk out tomorrow and marry the daughter of a clergyman or a dentist.' Aunt Prudence looked sternly at Mr Grimble as she said this, so that Gadberry wondered whether the old parasite was nursing improper ambitions in regard to a leash of great-grand-daughters of his own. He also wondered whether he, Gadberry, had an advantageous connection being cooked up for him by Aunt Prudence at this moment. Nothing, come to think of it, was more probable – and yet it was something which, until this moment, hadn't entered his head. For he was still a bit short, so to speak, in catching the wave-length of Aunt Prudence's distinctly dynastic and autocratic way of thinking. It was his sense of the old lady that he was fairly briskly advancing in her favour. Her increasing brusqueness (he was fairly sure) was in fact a sign of this. But perhaps he must reckon with the further fact that as one thus advanced in her good books one was expected to become more and more her creature. Certainly that was how Miss Bostock appeared to hold down her job. Feeling rather depressed again, Gadberry finished his Madeira. It didn't really go too well with roast turkey. He wondered whether any more liquor would be forthcoming during the latter part of this protracted meal.

'Boulter,' Mrs Minton said sharply, 'attend on Mr Nicholas. He may wish to give instructions on the wine.' She glanced round the table, and it was evident that she was very conscious of the portentous silence that this had produced. 'In future you are to take your station behind him.'

As Mrs Minton uttered these yet more staggering words, Gadberry was conscious of receiving a sharp blow on the side of his head. For a confused moment he rather supposed that Miss Bostock had relieved her feelings by the dramatic expedient of giving him a clip on the ear. She had merely, however, taken a rash jab at a roasted potato – virtually armour-plated, as roasted potatoes at Bruton tended to be – and inadvertently turned it into a projectile. And now her apology for this mishap struck Gadberry as merely formal, and indeed perfunctory. Mentally, he put a corroborative tick, so to speak, against his previously registered impression that Miss Bostock was an enemy. But if he found himself feeling uneasy – even a little dizzy – it wasn't because of anything of this kind. It came rather from a feeling that fortune's wheel had begun to revolve more rapidly than was comfortable. The only conceivable explanation of these changed dispositions at Mrs Minton's board was that she had made up her mind that his period of probation or apprenticeship at Bruton was over. He was on the up and up at such a pace that it seemed impossible that the mere momentum of the thing wouldn't take him flashing past his apex to return ruining into the gulfs below.

In this Gadberry had conceivably hit upon a merely superstitious reaction to what was happening. At the same time, if very obscurely, he was aware of the return of something like moral crisis. Keeping up his incredible imposture was a feat so crazy as to carry a kind of sustaining exhilaration along with it. He wasn't at all sure that he really wanted, on the other hand, to bring the deception definitively off. For one thing, a lifetime at Bruton – even with Miss Bostock sacked and Aunt Prudence herself departed to the shades – was a state of affairs he couldn't really see the shape of or get a feeling for. For another thing, the less he liked Mrs Minton (and he was coming to feel he didn't like her at all) the less did he want to gull and cheat her.

This was a paradox so odd that he could make nothing of it. But he was quite clear as to his central perception. To travel hopefully (which was what he had been doing) was rather fun. But he didn't terribly want to arrive. Perhaps – he told himself – he had been clinging in a muzzy way to the entirely untenable notion that what he was engaged upon was essentially an enormous practical joke. If Aunt Prudence were to die tomorrow (and why, with that shockingly bad heart, shouldn't she?) and he were to find himself her heir the day after, it wouldn't be at all easy to continue viewing his achievements in anything like that light. He, George Gadberry, so rationally ready to compound with fate for modest satisfactions, would in fact have become one of the big-time crooks of the century.

'Comberford? I think not.'

'What's that, Aunt Prudence?' Gadberry realised that he had been wool-gathering, so that the words just addressed to him were unintelligible. He glanced up the table at Mrs Minton as he spoke, and it struck him that she was returning his gaze with peculiar severity.

'I am saying, sir, that the sooner you cease to call yourself Nicholas Comberford the better. And I think you know why.'

10

Very naturally, the dizzy sensation that had lately assailed Gadberry returned upon him at this juncture with redoubled force. He was unmasked. Aunt Prudence – never to be Aunt Prudence again – had penetrated to his deception, and during this meal had been ministering to his fatuous sense of triumphant cunning only the more staggeringly to deliver this lethal blow. Gadberry wondered whether he should rise and make a dash for freedom. Boulter was portly and lumbering; Mr Grimble was in uncertain command of any bodily functions other than that of appetite; Dr Pollock looked scarcely formidable. He could make good at least the first stage of a getaway easily enough.

'Minton-Comberford is possible,' he heard Aunt Prudence saying. 'But Comberford-Minton is more euphonious. In the circumstances, moreover, I believe that it will be more correct.' Mrs Minton paused to pick up a glass of claret – for Boulter had now with admirable celerity provided this auxiliary beverage. 'Not that, at the moment, the matter can be absolutely determined upon. Comberford-Minton-Minton is another possibility. I shall not enter further into this at present. It would be inappropriate.' Mrs Minton glanced at Grimble, the Pollocks and Miss Bostock in turn, as if to underline the indisputable fact that these were persons whose humble station excluded them from taking any useful part in such deliberations. 'On the other hand,' Mrs Minton pursued, 'affability and condescension – social virtues the value of which my dear father early impressed upon me – prompt me to make an announcement upon this unassuming occasion. Nicholas – Nicholas Comberford-Minton-Minton, as he may have to become – is to be my heir. My man of

68

business is to wait upon me tomorrow, so that the necessary dispositions may be made. Meanwhile, I would ask you to drink to dear Nicholas' health.'

This was solemnly done. Gadberry, although his head was reeling, remembered to do most of the right things. They included shaking hands with Boulter – an obvious turn when affability and condescension were at a premium. With Aunt Prudence this went down very well, as did the suggestion that in the servants' hall the occasion should be celebrated by a moderate issue of small beer. Grimble had improved the occasion by securing the claret jug and contriving to hang on to it in a manner so suggestive of his sacerdotal functions that Boulter had rapidly to decant another couple of bottles. Mrs Pollock had gone into a kind of fawning routine which struck Gadberry as of a spine-chilling order. Dr Pollock, on the other hand, preserved a mildly ironical social competence which Gadberry liked better – although it prompted him, indeed, to make a mental note that here was somebody to keep a wary eye on. Miss Bostock produced conventional tokens of pleasure. The conventionality was unsurprising. At the same time, Gadberry was conscious of a lurking sense that the woman was *really* pleased. He found this perplexing. It didn't appear to be an evening upon which everything was coming her way.

The party presently settled down to consume trifle – a children's-party confection which Aunt Prudence had probably ordered as a dish appropriate upon occasions of high festivity. It would commonly have reeked of Australian sherry – only (as Gadberry suspected) the admirable Boulter had dug an unobtrusive hole in it and poured in half a bottle of brandy. Under the influence of this, and of a further couple of glasses of claret rapidly consumed, Gadberry began to feel quite cheerful. He *had* arrived; there was no more hopeful travelling to do; after some mumbo-jumbo with lawyers on the following day he would never be George Gadberry again. He wouldn't even be Nicholas Comberford. He would be Nicholas Comberford-Minton-Minton. He would have to *say* 'Comberford-Minton-Minton' whenever he was asked his name by a shopkeeper or a policeman.

This struck him (for the moment) as extremely funny. The thought of it carried comforting suggestions of that outsize practical joke. Not that the thought of a policeman was a particularly happy one. It engendered a lurking vision of *Comberford-Minton-Minton* making banner headlines in the national press in connection with something nasty transacting itself between the bench and the dock at the Old Bailey.

Despite this sobering reflection, Gadberry found himself, a few minutes later, getting the ladies out of the dining-room with the due authority of an heir. He summoned the gentleman to his either hand, preserving the proper manner of a junior who is also a host. When Boulter brought in coffee, he invited him to drink a glass of port before nodding to him to withdraw. For just a few minutes, he contrived a vision of himself as leading this sort of life for ever and ever.

It was difficult to tell whether the Reverend Mr Grimble had made much of what was going on. During the latter part of dinner, and from the point at which the claret had appeared, any residual coherence which his venerable condition had left in his conversation had rapidly attenuated itself. He was now contenting himself with an occasional malign mumble. At least Gadberry judged it to be malign – a conclusion reinforced by the equally occasional flashing out, above the bird's-nest beard, of a glance disconcertingly suggestive of gleeful cunning. It would have been almost possible to persuade oneself – Gadberry reflected – that Grimble was nursing the consciousness of some enormous practical joke on his own part. But that, of course, was impossible. That such a notion should come into Gadberry's head merely instanced the chronic suspiciousness which his peculiar situation prompted, and which had already been operative that evening in relation to Miss Bostock. Grimble was as witless as a dotard in an old play.

But at least he was aware of the weather. Having elicited from Boulter when handing the coffee that it was now snowing hard, he presently rose unsteadily to his feet with the announcement that he proposed to call the fly. The fly, Gadberry knew, was some species of superannuated horse-drawn vehicle to be hired in the village, and it seemed to him that he wasn't stretching his new status too far in immediately proposing to send the old gentleman home in one of the Abbey cars. Grimble, however, rejected this suggestion testily. He even refused to let the fly be telephoned for by a servant. All servants were unreliable nowadays, and he didn't want the job made a mess of. Nor would he hear of its being undertaken for him by his young host. He would make his way to the instrument himself. Having more or less intelligibly intimated this much, Grimble wandered round the dining-room, tried his best to quit it through a succession of cupboards, and then did eventually find the door and disappear.

'I say – do you think the old boy can really make a telephone call?' Gadberry put this to Dr Pollock rather as if seeking a professional opinion.

'It's not impossible. And, if he doesn't, we can sort the thing out later. The old value their independence, you know. One ought to think twice every time, before impairing their sense of it. And Grimble is laudably well able to look after himself.'

'But he wanders a bit in his mind, doesn't he? At matins last Sunday, for instance. He seemed to keep losing his place and repeating himself. We prayed three times for the High Court of Parliament. That can't have been right.'

'Perhaps he thinks this lot can do with all the intercession it's possible to muster up.' Pollock, who had lit a pipe, was chatting easily and in a tone of cool friendliness that Gadberry rather liked. Pollock didn't seem much impressed by the events of the evening. 'And I often notice method in Grimble's madness. For example, I'll bet you were out of church on the dot, as usual. If he repeats one thing, he omits another. So nobody much minds. And it wouldn't matter if they did – unless, of course, it was the Bishop.'

'Or Aunt Prudence.'

'Ah.' Pollock didn't take up this joke. 'Do you plan to spend most of your time at the Abbey? Let me congratulate you again, by the way, on what your great-aunt was telling us.'

'Yes, I expect I'll stay around a good deal. And thank you very much. But Aunt Prudence has been a bit precipitate, if you ask me. I seem to have been here a very short time, and I'd rather have had longer to play myself in.' Gadberry was conscious, as he made this speech, that it did, oddly enough, reflect his actual feelings.

'You must have been handling the bowling masterfully in the opening overs.' Pollock said this with the touch of irony he was apt to produce from time to time. This too Gadberry rather liked, but nevertheless it had an effect of setting him on his guard.

'I must seem an absolute fortune hunter, you know.' Gadberry had recourse to his ingenuous note. 'But the point is that there's pretty well nobody else. Both Mintons and Comberfords have become thin on the ground. Hence this business of the grand new surname, I suppose. But I just wish Aunt Prudence hadn't been in such a hurry. Of course, I can understand her motive.' Gadberry paused, fleetingly aware of indiscretion. 'She's all right, I suppose, on the mental side?'

'The mental side?' Pollock took his pipe from his mouth and glanced at Gadberry curiously.

'Well – I mean not going too much old Grimble's way. I do sometimes feel she's a bit odd. Seeming to think she lives in a society that vanished a century ago. And talking like a book in her great-grandfather's library. It worries me at times.'

'My dear Comberford, I wouldn't *worry*.' Pollock seemed amused. 'Mrs Minton is perfectly clear in her head. She knows just what she's doing. Even if there were much nearer relations, they wouldn't have a chance of going into court and successfully upsetting your apple-cart. Forgive me if I'm being too candid. It's a consideration it's perfectly natural and proper you should have in your head.'

'I see,' Gadberry said a little awkwardly. He supposed he *had* been fishing for something like this. 'Of course I'd be glad anyway that Aunt Prudence isn't going potty.'

'Well, she may be – at a reasonable sort of pace. I must admit that she has become a little more eccentric since I first came to the practice here. Later on, the process may be accelerated. In your new position, I feel it's proper you should be told this. You'll have to make any necessary arrangements, after all.' Pollock paused. 'I wonder where Grimble's got to? A single telephone call oughtn't to be taking all this time.'

'Perhaps I'd better go and see.' Gadberry half rose from his chair, and then suddenly sat down again. He was aware that something rather puzzling had turned up. 'But I'm not quite sure what you mean. About my great-aunt, that's to say.'

'You mustn't think it too sinister.' Pollock seemed aware that he must dish out what his profession terms reassurance. 'Plenty of the very old sink finally into senile dementia. It has it's painful side, of course. But nowadays we know how to handle these things pretty well. Particularly where money's no problem.'

'I see.' In point of fact, Gadberry's mind was beginning to grope in a great darkness. 'But Aunt Prudence's physical condition – well, isn't that relevant?'

'Extremely so, my dear Comberford. It's precisely what I'm saying. You must be aware, I suppose, that Mrs Minton has the typical physical constitution of a likely centenarian – the very type whose mind is bound to go long before her body. But I assure you this need occasion you no distress. Long-drawn-out terminal illness associated with physical pain and decay is far the more harrowing thing all round.'

'You mean that Aunt Prudence hasn't hurried on all this because she knows she's in a bad way – with a heart, or something like that?'

As he asked this question, Gadberry was aware that he had admitted into his voice inflections of the largest perturbation and dismay. It was scarcely surprising, therefore, that Dr Pollock was now looking at him very curiously indeed.

'A heart? Whatever should put that in your head? The old lady hasn't been telling you anything of the sort, surely? She doesn't strike me as likely to start imagining things about herself. She's simply not a hypochondriac type. Not that phobia about heart disease is all that rare.' Pollock was silent for a moment – perhaps, Gadberry thought, through embarrassment at finding himself in the presence of a young man who had demonstrably been nourishing baseless hopes about the speedy demise of a near relative. And now he spoke a trifle shortly. 'I'm your great-aunt's doctor,' he said, 'or what she would probably call her medical adviser. It wouldn't be proper for me to discuss her health in any detail. But what I've said, my dear man, I've said. She's as sound as a bell. Your anxieties – and you seem to go in for them in what is no doubt a very creditable way – are entirely beside the mark.'

'I'm very glad to hear it.' Gadberry, strangely enough, was able to say this with some sense of conviction. Long years with Aunt Prudence, it was true, constituted a vision he knew he simply couldn't dig. On the other hand, the fact that she could scarcely be said to possess an amiable personality hadn't resulted in his wishing her other than well. At least he found that he didn't in the least wish her ill. 'Shall we find Grimble,' he heard himself say, 'and think about joining the ladies?'

Gadberry licked a finger and thumb, and with a reasonably steady hand extinguished the half-dozen candles on the dinner-table. It occurred to him that Pollock's profession had probably given him a sufficiently disenchanted view of human nature to cause him to think little of what had occurred. But with Gadberry himself it was a different matter. It wasn't simply as one cheated of the speedy expectation of an inheritance that he was disconcerted. In fact it wasn't as that at all. He was experiencing, once more, that nasty feeling of being a prominent actor in an increasingly unintelligible play. And it was a play, he suspected, now rapidly approaching its denouement.

11

There was nothing modish about the general decor of Bruton Abbey. The fabric was mediaeval, with bits and pieces added by eminent eighteenth-century architects in the Picturesque Taste. The furniture, for some mysterious reason to which Gadberry had not yet succeeded in penetrating, was almost exclusively Victorian. The pictures, of which there were a great many, ran to nothing – Gadberry had sometimes reflected – which would have appeared out of the way to his former landlady Mrs Lapin herself. Apart from a startlingly indecent nude by Etty which hung bang over the drawing-room chimney piece, most appeared to be by Landseer in his vein as a celebrant of the indigenous fauna of Great Britain. The Abbey being, moreover, in some disrepair, and thus affording easy ingress to the actual brute creation, these mute representations were sometimes oddly reinforced from without. It was quite common to come upon an owl perched above a Monarch of the Glen, or a couple of bats depending from the frame of some murkily evoked rural scene. In places, indeed, it might have been possible to suppose that Mrs Minton had gone in for certain decorative notions of a modern and ephemeral sort, as when interior walls were discovered to be clothed in matted growths of ivy. These irruptions of wild nature were the odder when one reflected that they couldn't conceivably be a consequence of penury. They must simply be part of Mrs Minton's conception of a feudal order of things to which she subscribed.

In the cloisters now there was an eerie light reflected from the snow beginning to silt up outside, and through some open or broken casement flakes were floating in with sufficient freedom to be falling damply on one's face as one walked. And everywhere there was a sufficient effect of moaning, rattling and creaking to suggest that quite a gale was blowing up.

Conducting Dr Pollock through these dismal effects, the spurious Nicholas Comberford recalled gloomily his authentic counterpart's having remarked that Bruton Abbey enjoyed a somewhat remote situation. It was certainly true. The tiny village of Bruton was a mile away, and apart from this there was nothing within walking distance except monotonous stretches of moor. Gadberry, for long a dweller in cities, had only to think of it to feel very lonesome indeed.

But at present he had a different preoccupation. It had been strange enough that Comberford had proved totally misinformed in the matter of his great-aunt's attitude to alcohol. It was very much stranger that he had been equally astray as to her state of health. He had declared categorically that she was in an advanced stage of heart disease – and now here was Dr Pollock, who must know, laughing such an idea out of court. But *must* Pollock know? Was it possible that the old lady was really very ill, and had for some reason successfully concealed the fact from the local doctor?

Gadberry, as he made a detour in search of the missing Grimble, considered this supposition on its merits. But of course it *had* no merits. For one thing, as soon as you really thought of the matter, you realised that a mortally sick woman was about the last thing that Aunt Prudence corresponded to. For another thing –

Here Gadberry broke off, for a consideration of the utmost simplicity had suddenly occurred to him. The real Comberford had been in no position to entertain any confident knowledge about his great-aunt's state of health. Until the receipt of her letter proposing that he should domesticate himself at Bruton there had been no suggestion that he had held any recent communication with her. So how could he have the intimate information he had claimed?

The Abbey was not, at this time of year, a place in which it was at all easy to feel suddenly cold. But Gadberry felt just this now. For he realised – and he acknowledged to himself that it was a realisation pitifully belated – that Comberford was a shocking liar, and that the whole business of Mrs Minton's brief expectation of life had been fed to him simply to make her relative's extraordinary proposal appear a little more attractive than it would otherwise have been. Big money from the conspiracy, and big money in reasonable time, would have appeared to Comberford his strongest card, and he had led with it straightaway. Really and truly, big money had been only an uncertain prospect a long way ahead.

This was what it was now, despite Gadberry's spectacular promotion of only an hour ago. A half-share in £5,000 a year might still be what his efforts were pulling in when Mrs Minton was celebrating her hundredth birthday. What was more, it would be all that Comberford in his Riviera seclusion was pulling in too. There was something puzzling about the whole thing.

The suspicion that he had been cheated – that his own imposture was conducting itself, so to speak, inside another one in which he himself was the dupe – didn't, Gadberry found, very much annoy him in itself. He didn't feel morally outraged by his discovery; indeed, there would have been a certain unreasonableness in a reaction of that sort, since any such situation placed him, after all, in the role of the biter bit, and one mustn't expect honour among thieves. There was a sense in which he was even relieved, since Mrs Minton's death – or so he had been coming to think – must finally and fatally involve him in permanent deception on an intimidating scale. In this feeling he was again, perhaps, up against a magical sense of the thing. His present situation could be viewed as a fantastic lark. But there was a kind of death in the notion that never in life could plain George Gadberry – but also talented George Gadberry, for had he not enjoyed that big success in *The Rubbish Dump?* – bob up again.

Of course Gadberry could, he supposed, bob up again *now*. All that was necessary was the resolution to make a clean break. He had only to pack a small bag, stuff his pockets with as much cash as his own sporadically operative conscience would permit, and hasten away from Bruton through its rising winds and falling snows. Out, out into the storm: such a departure would have a certain theatrical quality that made an appeal to him. He might even accomplish the initial stage of his flight here and now by commandeering Mr Grimble's fly.

At this moment Mr Grimble made his appearance again. He seemed to have been straying around the imperfectly enclosed cloisters for some time. Snow was sprinkled on his shoulders and the rime sparkled in his beard. He would have looked like Father Christmas if there hadn't been something about him more suggestive of an imp or troll. He greeted Gadberry with a cackle of laughter, and with a gleeful rubbing together of his hands which, although no doubt no more than a precautionary measure against frostbite, somehow conveyed an impression of cunning which Gadberry didn't like. Quite unreasonably, Gadberry found himself rather frightened of this disagreeable but presumably harmless old creature.

'Did you get through, sir?' he asked solicitously. He had a notion that it especially became the heir of Bruton to adopt a deferential attitude towards a dependant so venerably advanced as Grimble within the vale of years.

'Everything is in train, Comberford, everything is in train.' Something sinister about the manner in which Grimble said this was enhanced – or perhaps it was merely suggested – by a particularly desperate hooting-act put on at this moment by one of the Abbey's resident owls. For all its feathers – Gadberry supposed – the creature was a-cold. 'In train, I say, in train,' Grimble repeated. His frosted breath hung around like a miasma. The temperature must be dropping like a stone. Grimble seemed aware of the phenomenon himself. 'This place is too cold for hell,' he said, and walked on.

Boulter, who had a commendable instinct to achieve some effect of sanity in those spheres of Bruton life that lay within his province, had contrived in the drawing-room a fire before which it would have been perfectly feasible to roast an ox. Unfortunately most of the heat that didn't go straight up the chimney made its way into the dim vaulting that hung overhead. Had it been possible for the company to levitate to this region and conduct their post-prandial civilities while hovering thirty feet above the floor, it was conceivable that quite a cosy hour might have been the result. As it was, Mrs Minton's household and her guests became progressively numb and dumb. Perhaps, Gadberry thought, a certain amount of conversation was actually being produced, only to be congealed at the point of utterance. Perhaps, as in Baron Münchausen's narrative, a thaw would one day release it, and there would be a babble of inane chatter in the empty room.

Meantime, he had leisure to continue to picture himself as fled into the storm. There appeared to be no reason why he could not make a quick end of the whole business. If he simply vanished, he supposed, it might be assumed that he had met with some misadventure or accident, and a vexatious pursuit might ensue. But why shouldn't he, in his character as Nicholas Comberford, leave a note saying that he couldn't stand the place, and that if Mrs Minton wanted an heir she must try again? If he'd really had as much as he could take, or if he was prompted to act decisively in terms of that obscure recurrent alarm occasioned in him by a sense of unknown factors in his situation, then giving mortal offence in this fashion was undoubtedly the easiest way out. Mrs Minton, one could be sure, far from attempting to recall him, would never mention the name of her great-nephew Nicholas again.

But the trouble about this was that it really wouldn't be a nice thing to do. Aunt Prudence was in various ways an intolerable old person, but as far as he himself was concerned there was no denying that she deserved well of him. If she liked anybody in the world, it was clearly the young man who was in fact sheltering beneath her roof (if sheltering, indeed, it could be called in this temple of the winds or palace of ice) as a consequence of gross imposture. To bolt – certainly to bolt after having left some nasty message as a parting shot – would be to do rather more than simply let Aunt Prudence down. It would be to bite the hand that fed him, and that had just made the gesture of proposing to feed him a great deal more.

Confronted with this paradox of his situation, Gadberry felt a good deal discouraged. His chronic sense of the perplexing character of the moral universe descended upon him heavily. Moreover there was the awkward fact that, just as he had only a vaguely massive notion of the threat he wanted to bolt *from*, so he had no clear idea of any prospect he could now bolt *to*. He could, indeed, take money with him, so that he would be all right for a time. But what about after that? He would once more be George Gadberry, but he wasn't very sure that he could live as George Gadberry had lived. He was like a wild creature which, after even a short period of captivity, has no clear memory of what wild nature feels like.

The party dragged on for a further gloomy half-hour, after which the Pollocks got up to go away. So thick was the snow outside, however, that their actual departure was delayed while one of the outdoor servants fitted certain clanking mediaeval contraptions, known as the chains, to the back wheels of their car. The operation was unfamiliar to Gadberry, who nevertheless felt that he must superintend it with an air of rural expertise, so that in the result he was blue and shivering by the time the doctor and his wife departed into the blizzard. Then Grimble had to be fed into the fly, the fly's driver dug out of the kitchens to which he had repaired, and the fly's motive power to be lashed and cajoled into a sufficient state of equine animation to trundle the conveyance down the drive. By the time these evolutions were concluded Gadberry felt fit for nothing but bed.

He returned to the drawing-room, however, if only with the idea of making sure that the place wasn't going to be burnt down – or even, perhaps, out of a kind of dumb sense that a deft kick or two at Boulter's enormous embers might really produce in the small hours a conflagration in which Bruton Abbey, hitherto more or less inviolate through the centuries, would disappear for ever. As it turned out, this wouldn't have been possible. Mrs Minton was still in the room, seated in a chair on one side of the fireplace. As Miss Bostock was arranging her footstool, it was to be presumed that she had just taken her place there. And there was an empty chair opposite her. Gadberry, who didn't like the look of this, spoke a shade hastily.

'My dear aunt, I'm sure you must be very tired. Perhaps you should – '

'Pray do not speculate, Nicholas, on what I ought, or ought not, to do. Nor need you to be so irrational as to claim assurance in regard to the subjective sensations of another. And now sit down. I have something to communicate to you. But, first, place a chair for Miss Bostock. Bostock, I wish you to hear what I have to say.'

12

'In the course of tomorrow morning,' Mrs Minton began, 'Mr Middleweek will call. He is, as you know, my solicitor, and it is my intention that a number of documents shall be executed in the course of our interview. It is not, I need hardly say, merely a matter of a will – as it doubtless would be were Miss Bostock, say, desirous of settling her affairs. It is only for the poor that matters are as simple as that. Nicholas – you follow me?'

'Well, yes – I suppose I do.'

'If certain iniquities in the present laws governing death duties and the like are to be defeated, it is requisite that various dispositions of property should be made at a date which shall subsequently prove to have been not less than seven years before my own demise. This does not mean, Nicholas, that you will assume control of anything more than the modest allowance at present made to you. There will be trustees, and so forth. I ought to add, moreover, that I have no intention of dying within the next seven years. Nothing of the sort is in my mind. So there is not, in fact, any hurry. I wish, however, that these dispositions should be made now. The reason for this I shall presently communicate to you. Once more, you follow me?'

'Yes, I think I do.' Gadberry, who ought to have been all agog at this point, found himself feeling merely uncomfortable. 'But need you tell me all this just at – ?'

'Nicholas, you are developing a bad habit of offering me what you appear to regard as your own better wisdom on the manner of my conducting my affairs. Pray allow me to continue. I wish these matters to be understood clearly. Bostock, if I am *not* clear, you are to say so.'

'Then I think you ought to be a little more specific now.' Miss Bostock, although existing in a depressed station of life, commonly addressed her employer with some briskness. 'Is Mr Comberford to understand that, in the event of your being quite mistaken as to your expectation of life, trustees would take over where you left off?'

'Certainly not. As I understand these rather intricate matters, the trustees are created merely as the formal custodians of various properties during my lifetime. Were I to die next week – which I repeat I do not intend to do – their functions would lapse at once. There would be disastrous estate duties and so forth. But Nicholas would come immediately into his inheritance.'

'That is clear,' Miss Bostock said. She gave Gadberry one of her steady looks. 'I am sure that Mr Comberford takes the point very well.'

Gadberry found this disagreeable, although he wasn't quite sure why. He ought at least to be making a careful mental note of it all, if only to report to the authentic Comberford when he chose to make contact again. But he still just wanted to go to bed. He tried, therefore, to speed up this nocturnal conference.

'Well, then,' he said, 'why do you want to fix things tomorrow?'

'Because I have arranged a luncheon party, Nicholas. The Shilbottles are coming, and it is possible – indeed likely – that Arthur Shilbottle may wish to know how the land lies.'

'Oh, the Shilbottles. Yes, of course.' Gadberry performed a rapid mental consultation of the late Magnus Minton's *Memoirs*, but without result. 'That will be very nice.'

'I cannot see that you are in a position to form such a judgment. The Shilbottles are surely unknown to you as yet. Indeed, I do not possess their familiar acquaintance myself. As you must be aware, the Marquis of Aydon's estates lie in Northumberland. Lord Arthur Shilbottle, who is his younger brother, has only recently acquired properties in our neighbourhood – and only, I may add, as a consequence of his marriage. Lady Arthur has lately inherited a large fortune. I understand it may be termed a *very* large fortune. Lady Arthur is of American extraction, but is nevertheless substantially presentable. And the daughters have been accorded an upbringing entirely suitable to English gentlewomen.'

'I'm very glad to hear it.' Gadberry made this imbecile reply out of considerable perturbation of mind. It didn't take much acuteness to see where all this was heading for. It was the Court page of *The Times*, morning clothes, grey toppers, whole barns and granaries piled with wedding presents, and a marriage ceremony performed – no doubt – by the Archbishop of York. All this had lately been hovering in a nightmarish fashion in Gadberry's consciousness. Here it really was.

'Did you say something about daughters?' he asked. He might as well know the worst at once.

'Of course they are coming to lunch with us too. Alethea and Anthea. I may say that I have already had some conversation with Shirley Shilbottle.'

'Shirley?'

'Shirley is Lady Arthur Shilbottle. I agree that as a girl's Christian name Shirley scarcely commends itself. However, it possibly commemorates some kinship with the Ferrers, who were earls of Derby in the thirteenth century, and must be considered as of respectable antiquity. You will recall that Laurence Shirley, who was, I think, the fourth earl, was the last English nobleman to suffer a felon's death. He drove to Tyburn in his own carriage, and was hanged with a silken rope. This seems to make a connection with the American colonies the more probable.'

'It clearly does.' Gadberry was by now well practised in receiving this sort of thing. 'But why should you already have had some conversation with Lady Arthur?'

'My dear Nicholas, I am, as you know, a woman of a liberal turn of mind. In the sphere which we are now considering. I cannot but act in a spirit of the greatest tolerance. The miseries of enforced marriage, as the old phrase has it, shall never be laid at my door – in relation to a young man that is to say, for it is entirely proper that a girl should marry precisely according to her parents' wish. But a young man, I repeat, must not be constrained. Particularly if he is of good family, and so possessed of those qualities of manliness and independence which only a distinguished lineage can confer.'

'I'm sure that's absolutely right.' Gadberry almost blushed as he said this, for he was quite clear the old woman was talking the most awful rot. 'That sort of young man must be let marry the girl he fancies.'

Mrs Minton looked displeased.

'Nicholas, you are being foolish again. It is precisely his possibly behaving in that manner that I was reprehending in young Tony Hartley. What my liberal principles require me to assert is the necessity of *choice* – of perfectly *free* choice. And this is why I had to make quite sure. Fortunately, matters are entirely propitious. Lady Arthur, who controls her own fortune, is definite about it. Alethea and Anthea are to be treated strictly as co-heiresses. It is the American custom, no doubt.'

'So that's my free choice – between the Hon. Alethea and the equally Hon. Anthea?'

'Pray do not be facetious, Nicholas – and particularly on such a serious subject as that of styles and titles. But you are correct as to the fact.'

'What if these Shilbottles now have a son?'

'It is a question you do very well to ask.' Mrs Minton directed upon Gadberry one of those glances of high approval which were apt to disconcert him more than was anything else. 'But Shirley Shilbottle is definitely beyond the child-bearing age, and any subsequent marriage by Arthur Shilbottle is neither here nor there. The money – or rather the land, since to talk about money is decidedly vulgar – is Shirley's. Every penny of it. I mean, every acre.'

'I see. So it's pretty well in the bag?'

'The expression is unfamiliar to me, Nicholas. But if its import is as I suppose, I give an affirmative answer with confidence.'

'And tomorrow's the day? I line them up and choose – like oranges and lemons?'

'My dear Nicholas, of course *les convenances* must be observed. Even if your preference instantly becomes clear to you, you will upon this first occasion continue to be equally attentive to both girls. On a second meeting you may, however, make some proposal to one of them alone.'

'A proposal of marriage, you mean?'

'Certainly not. A proposal to go riding together, or something of the sort. After that, there should be some slight further delay. I should be inclined to say that your passion may quite properly declare itself in about three or four weeks' time. And now, as that is settled, I will go to bed.'

In accordance with a custom which had established itself at the Abbey, Gadberry now conducted Aunt Prudence ceremoniously to her own apartments. When he returned to the drawing-room to turn out the lights – for Boulter was to be presumed by now to have signed off for the night – he found to his surprise that Miss Bostock was still in possession of it. This hadn't happened before. Indeed Gadberry had a notion that *les convenances* as recently evoked were dead against it. Unmarried ladies quartered in country houses never sit up with the gentlemen unchaperoned. Or at least they don't do so (unless they are very fast) in Victorian novels of high life. And current mores at Bruton Abbey appeared to hitch on more or less to that. But certainly Miss Bostock wasn't discomposed. She made no move to withdraw. Instead, she sat tight, and gave Gadberry one of her celebrated looks. It was a look that didn't seem to search into his heart so much as into his pockets; she might have been estimating to what extent he had loaded these with the Minton spoons and forks.

'Sit down,' Miss Bostock said.

Gadberry sat down – not without resenting something decidedly peremptory in Miss Bostock's tone. Of course, one had to make allowances for the woman. To live in a household where the servants were required to address you as 'Madam' but where they regularly heard you addressed as 'Bostock' by your employer: this was something which would surely in time sour any temper. But she and

Gadberry were, to some extent, fellow sufferers, after all. It was unreasonable that they should be at feud with one another. Gadberry decided to have another go at being conciliatory now. So he once more put on his ingenuous act.

'I say,' he began, 'that was a bit of a facer, wasn't it? Free choice, indeed! Still, I suppose one is bound to prove more attractive than the other.'

'I think not.'

'Oh come, Miss Bostock! *Less un*attractive than the other if you like. I've got to look on the bright side, after all.'

'There is no bright side, there are only two identical sides.'

'I don't understand what you mean.'

'Mrs Minton has a sense of humour, has she not, Mr Comberford?'

'I can't say I've much noticed it.'

'Well, she has. But it is of a grim and private sort. In this last conversation, and while offering you your pick, as it were, between the two Shilbottle girls, she suppressed one relevant fact. They are identical twins, and it is impossible to distinguish between them.'

13

If this was really a joke, Gadberry didn't think much of it. In fact he felt almost unreasonably angry – partly with Miss Bostock, whose manner he increasingly didn't like, and partly with Mrs Minton, who suddenly stood revealed to him as unbearably arrogant and tiresomely mad. Of course he had really known the worst about Mrs Minton for some time, and it had been sheer weakness to dodge a consciousness of the fact simply because he had got into her good graces. Objectively regarded, it was humiliating that he had succeeded in this way, since it was something, surely, that only a horrid young toady could do.

'It's ridiculous!' he said. 'And it's disgusting, too.'

'Disgusting?' There was something peculiarly insulting in the manner in which Miss Bostock contrived to repeat this word. She might have been implying that Gadberry was one from whom it fell quaintly and surprisingly – as it might do from some humble creature dislodged from beneath a stone.

'Yes, disgusting. Having two indistinguishable girls – if they're really that – '

'They certainly are.'

'Very well. Having them driven into a pound, and being told to choose one or the other.'

'You mean it would be less disgusting if they were quite different?'

'Of course it would.' Gadberry said this with conviction. It was something he was quite clear about, although he didn't know why.

'Then perhaps you had better refrain from making advances to either of them.'

'That's exactly what I will do.'

'Mrs Minton – who has just treated you so munificently – will scarcely be pleased.'

'Oh, to hell with Mrs Minton! I've had enough.'

There was a silence – a silence into which one of the Bruton owls deftly dropped a particularly spine-chilling hoot. But to Gadberry it came with the effect of a triumphant paean. He had burnt his boats. In the words of the poet, the loathsome mask had fallen.

But something had gone wrong. Miss Bostock didn't seem at all shocked. Only her eyes had narrowed.

'No,' she said, 'that won't do.'

'What do you mean? What won't do?'

'Well – for a start, just rejecting the Misses Shilbottle. But how is your delicacy to be respected? You won't choose *one*. You can't marry *both*. Do you know, I can see only one solution?'

'I don't care twopence for your solution. I tell you, I'm packing in the whole – '

'I consider my solution extremely simple and elegant. You shall marry one Miss Shilbottle, and the real Nicholas Comberford can have the other.'

This time the silence was prolonged. It was also hideous to Gadberry's shattered sense. Miss Bostock sat gazing absently into the dying fire. Her attitude suggested no hint of drama. She might just have been feeling that things were growing duller even than before, and that she had better give up the day as a lost cause and get off to bed.

These appearances, disconcerting in themselves, came for some moments to Gadberry only confusedly and as if from a long way off. His mind was behaving like a television set in some advanced stage of electronic disease. Images flapped and flickered in it, dissolved into a grey chaos, formed again uncertainly as if behind some undulating flood. Then, rather to his surprise, he heard himself producing articulate speech.

'How did you know?' His voice was at once hoarse and trembling. 'How did you find out?'

'Know…find out?' Miss Bostock removed her gaze from the fire and fixed it on Gadberry. But now it seemed not hostile, but only puzzled and a little alarmed.

'That I'm not Comberford. Who told you? Was it Comberford himself? Are you two in on something together?' This time, Gadberry was just aware that he was shouting – or perhaps it was screaming. The woman had unnerved him completely.

'Not Comberford? Mr Comberford, I don't understand you at all. I think you must be tired. Perhaps – '

'Damn you!' Gadberry found that he had jumped to his feet and was waving his arms foolishly. 'You said that the real Nicholas Comberford could have one of those girls.'

'Mr Comberford, you are ill.' Miss Bostock spoke gently and solicitously – a thing monstrous and unnatural in itself. 'I have judged you to be a little strained for some time. And now you are imagining things. It is a delirium. Pray heaven that your mind isn't giving way.'

'I tell you, you said – '

'Dr Pollock will have got home by now. But he must return at once. I will telephone.'

Gadberry stared in stark horror at Miss Bostock. For a moment he believed what she said. The things he had heard her utter she hadn't uttered at all. He had gone mad.

Convinced of this, Gadberry sank into his chair again. He burst into tears.

'Good,' Miss Bostock said calmly. 'Now, my friend, we can talk.'

Gadberry shivered all over. He realised that what this hideous woman had said she *had* said. He had suffered no hallucination. She *did* know. The turn she had put on had been merely an ingenious trick to break his nerve. And it had succeeded – for a moment. But she damned well wasn't going to have it all her own way. He'd fight back – *now*.

'Very well.' Gadberry sat up and straightened his shoulders. 'We'll talk. And it's interesting that you *want* to talk. It's interesting you haven't sent for the police. In fact, you're in this for what you can get.'

'Now you *are* talking.' Miss Bostock nodded approvingly. 'I'll be surprised if we don't get along famously.'

'I still want to know how you found out. What did I do wrong?'

'Nothing *very* wrong, I'd say.' Miss Bostock appeared to consider the question dispassionately. 'But everything a little wrong. That's almost inevitable.'

'I suppose it is. But I don't see why you in particular – '

'A certain professional expertness was involved, young man. But never mind that. There's a much more important question – and it's for me to put it to you. Where is the real Nicholas Comberford?'

'I don't know.'

'Ah!' Without haste, Miss Bostock got to her feet, picked up a poker, and stirred the embers to a quick flare. 'Does he exist?'

'Of course he exists. How can I be a false Comberford if there isn't a true one?'

'Does he *still* exist? You haven't made away with him?'

'Made away with him!' Gadberry stared at Miss Bostock in simple astonishment. 'How could I have made away with him?'

'It's the natural presumption. By the way, what's your real name?'

'I won't tell you.'

'You will quite soon. But never mind that now. The obvious way of reading the facts is this: you have murdered Comberford and taken his place. Otherwise, he'd be here himself, happily collecting his inheritance.'

'It isn't so. Comberford's alive. Only – '

'But you say you don't know where he is. That means you couldn't produce him if you had to. What would a judge and jury, I wonder, think of *that*? I doubt whether they'd be troubled by the fact that the police couldn't produce the body.'

'You're trying to frighten me. Just as you did a few minutes ago, pretending I'd gone mad.'

'My dear young man, it's the facts that are frightening you. And well they may. By the way, you must have an uncanny resemblance to the real Nicholas. Are you an illegitimate brother or something?'

'I'm – ' Almost in the vein of Mrs Minton herself, Gadberry was about to assert the honourable lineage of the Gadberrys. But he had the wit to realise that this would be a mistake. He mustn't trade a scrap of information to this woman without some exchange in the shape of security in one form or another. 'I may be,' he said, 'or I may not. That's all for you to find out.'

'Is that kind of attitude going to take us far?' Miss Bostock glanced almost indulgently at Gadberry. 'And far, you know, is precisely where we have to get ourselves taken. This thing isn't nearly as simple as you seem to have been imagining. You've had all the luck for a start, but nothing's yet in the bag. And it isn't going to be tomorrow either, however many documents your supposed great-aunt signs for Mr Middleweek. The hazards go on and on and on. Let's make no mistake about that.'

'When I said I'm going to pack it in I meant it. And not just because you've found me out. The whole thing's too stupid. I don't want to end my life as a Minton-Minton, or whatever it is, married to a Shilbottle-Shilbottle. Mind you, I don't think there's anything particularly wrong about it. The idea was to give satisfaction all round. But it's not going to give *me* any satisfaction. I'd rather be navvying. I've done it before.'

'Your eyes, in fact, are opened?'

'Just that.'

'Then you'd better close them again. You see, you can't get away.'

'Yes I can. I can go back to being who I really am.'

'I don't think so. I agree that as the authentic Nicholas Comberford you could simply clear out. The police would have no interest in tracing you, for you wouldn't have broken the law. But once they'd been told you were an impostor – told by me, for example – they just wouldn't let the trail go. They'd find you, all right.'

Gadberry was silent. He saw that this was true. The dreadful woman had the whip hand of him. And she was going to use him for her own purposes.

'Look,' he said. 'There's really very little in this. That's where I've been sold. The old woman's going to live till she's a hundred. Your share would be no more than pin money. It certainly wouldn't be worth the risk of your becoming an accomplice in a conspiracy. You'd better forget about your precious discovery, and just let me quit.'

'I seem to remember that Mrs Minton rebuked you this evening for teaching other people their business. And it does seem to be a weakness of yours. I think you'd better go and sleep on the whole thing. Your position has its hazards, I agree. But it also has possibilities that you don't seem to have got the hang of. Perhaps you'll be clearer-headed when you wake up.' Miss Bostock, who had continued standing before the dying fire, now moved towards the door. 'Certainly we'll have another quiet chat quite soon. Good night.'

For some time Gadberry sat staring blindly into the dying fire. He didn't stir even when the bats (who usually took possession of the drawing-room at about this hour) began resentful manoeuvres in the vaulting. It was only when an extreme chill had overtaken him that he dragged himself to his feet, turned off the lights, and left the room. In the cloisters there was even more rattling and banging going on than before, for the wind was now rising to a gale. He could hear it whistling and roaring in the ruins of the Abbey church to the north of the house. It might have been a pack of wild creatures that was in synod there. Savage howlings filled the sacred choirs.

Something stirred in the shadows ahead of him as he began to make his way to his room. It was probably no more than one of the Abbey's ghosts, so he paid no attention. Indeed, being fed up with Bruton he was fed up with its sideshows as well, and in no mood to be respectful to some monkish figment. Coming up with this appearance, he steered a course straight through it. But this act of disrespect didn't come off. Gadberry found that he had bumped into Boulter, who was in consequence making dignified apologies in a justifiably reproachful tone.

This was an alarming encounter. Gadberry had supposed that Boulter, with the rest of the household, had withdrawn long ago to whatever obscure quarters were his. Perhaps he had been eavesdropping on that ghastly interview with Miss Bostock. Perhaps, in consequence, here was somebody else now in on his guilty secret.

'Security, sir,' Boulter said – as if it had occurred to him that he ought to justify his prowling presence. 'It poses its problems at Bruton, and particular in inclement weather. I could wish that Mrs Minton would install an efficient modern system of burglar-alarms. It may be done one day.'

Gadberry received this unenthusiastically. It referred, he supposed, to his own future proprietorship of the Abbey. And that was something that just wasn't going to happen now. He was going to employ all his cunning to get away. After that, an army of burglars was welcome to the lot.

'Boulter, I suppose you know the Shilbottles?' It wasn't quite clear to Gadberry why he asked this, since the subject didn't in the least interest him. But the sudden encounter with Boulter was an awkward one, and he had spoken more or less at random.

'Certainly, sir. I understand that the family is coming to luncheon tomorrow.'

'What are the daughters like?'

'Very pleasant young ladies, sir. Very pleasant young ladies, indeed. I understand their main interest to be the breeding of dogs. Rather large dogs. Bloodhounds and St Bernards, I have been given to understand. But then the Misses Shilbottle are rather large themselves. Yes, sir – well-built girls.'

'Are they good-looking?'

'I would hardly venture to assert so. It could not readily be claimed that they are well favoured, sir. "Homely" would be the appropriate expression. And the word would be employed rather in its American than in its English signification.'

'I see. Well, good night, Boulter.'

'Good night, sir.'

Gadberry moved off. It might be fair to say that he shuffled off, for his gait reflected his dispirited condition. Then another and more sensible topic of inquiry struck him, and he turned round.

'I say – Boulter!'

'Yes, sir?'

'How long has Miss Bostock been about the place?'

'Off hand, sir, I should estimate the period at about five years.'

'Don't you think it extraordinary that any woman would want to hold down such a job for all that time?'

'I'm sure it is not for me to say, sir.' Boulter's features had taken on the wooden expression of an offended servant.

'Well – dash it, man – you know what I mean.'

'I confess that I have an inkling, sir.' Boulter allowed himself a little to thaw – which was handsome of him, considering the air temperature at which this untimely colloquy was being conducted.

'She's a ghastly woman, you know.'

'That must be as you say, sir.' Not unnaturally, Boulter withdrew again into a discreet reserve. At the same time, he was looking at Gadberry a little oddly. But Gadberry wasn't disconcerted; for the present, at least, he was past caring whether his conduct appeared bizarre or not.

'Where did she come from, anyway?' he asked. 'How did ... did my great-aunt pick her up?'

'I have been given to understand, sir, that Miss Bostock was formerly in the police.'

'The police?' It was with a kind of nervous jump that Gadberry repeated this. 'What awful nonsense! Policewomen, or whatever they are called, just don't become ladies' companions. The idea simply isn't sensible.'

'It carries an element of surprise, sir, I don't doubt. But I understand that Miss Bostock was some way up in her branch of the constabulary. And she is, of course, a gentlewoman, although in reduced circumstances. Mrs Minton could not otherwise be expected to –'

'Yes, of course. But what reduced the woman's circumstances, if she was doing well as a female dick?'

'It is not for me to gossip, sir.'

'Oh, rot, Boulter.'

'Well, sir, I admit that your position has become one in which you are entitled to any information which may affect the future good name of the family.'

'That's right, Boulter. The Comberford-Mintons-Mintons, and all that.'

'Precisely, sir.' Boulter gave Gadberry another odd look. 'It is my impression, then, that Miss Bostock left the Force under a cloud.'

'I'll bet she did.'

'I imagine it to have been a matter, sir, of injudicious collaboration in some enterprise not wholly without a criminal aspect. It is curious that Mrs Minton should then have taken her into employment. But Mrs Minton is a remarkable woman, a very remarkable woman, indeed. I am sure you will agree with me.'

'Yes, Boulter, of course. So Miss Bostock was found out?'

'Just that, sir. It is the common fate of fraud and imposition, one is thankful to say. As the proverb has it, the mills of the law grind slowly, but they grind exceeding small.'

'Isn't it the mills of God?'

'It is precisely the same thing, sir, if we are right-thinking people. But if I may make the suggestion, it would be reasonable that we should severally retire.'

'Yes, of course.' Gadberry found that he was speaking out of a kind of daze. This last information about Miss Bostock was striking him as quite disproportionally ominous. 'But would you leave a message, Boulter, for whichever of the maids is about first? I'd like to be called early. I have …well, I have rather a lot of work to get through.'

'Quite so, sir.' Boulter's tone indicated a respectful acknowledgement of the burdens that must now fall on the heir of Bruton. About his glance, however, there was still something that was distinctly uncomfortable. 'I shall certainly see to it. Good night.'

14

It was long before Gadberry went to sleep that night. But as his thoughts were tedious and unprofitable to himself as they occurred, it is not likely that they would interest others. He did eventually pass into slumber – yet only to suffer – seemingly again and again, with no more than minor modifications – a dream by which he had not been troubled since his early days at the Royal Academy of Dramatic Art. He was on-stage, and he kept drying up. His lines just wouldn't come to him; he missed cue after cue; the prompter whispered to him in vain; his fellow actors performed prodigies of improvisation on his behalf, inventing whole loops of dialogue that should have enabled him to collect his scattered wits and take up the thread again. Yet it was all to no purpose. He had an uncertain notion that what he was involved in was a play of Shakespeare's, but all that would come into his head was Shakespeare's own words for his situation:

> As an unperfect actor on the stage,
> Who with his fear is put beside his part…

That was exactly it, and there he was in the middle of some incomprehensible action, which went on and on forever, with the curtain obstinately refusing to come down on it.

But suddenly the curtain *did* come down. Or rather it had become a different sort of curtain, and something quite familiar was happening to it. It was his bedroom curtain; a housemaid was drawing it back upon a wintry scene; the tray with his early-morning tea was already standing by his bedside.

Gadberry glanced at his watch, and saw that it was just seven o'clock. Boulter had taken him at his word. Then the housemaid turned round, and he saw that she was very young, very pretty, and at the same time somebody of so lowly a station on the Bruton domestic staff that he had never seen her before. Presumably she had to get up before anybody else. Her first job was probably to take tea to Boulter, just as she had now brought tea to him.

Making for the door, the young person quite distinguishably moderated her pace. Cautiously – but again *quite* distinguishably – she smiled at Gadberry. She was bright-eyed with the consciousness that here was a tremendous frolic. She was all for being grabbed, kissed, and for some moments tumbled more or less innocently on the bed before asserting her virginal status and escaping amid giggles from the room. Gadberry was mortified to find that he took no interest whatever in this wholesome proposal. He just hadn't the heart for it. Yet only the evening before he had been able to indulge at least in a little harmless bath-time fantasy of this sort. Now he was only able to say 'Thank you' in an elderly sort of way and watch this delightful girl depart disappointed. It just showed how his darkening prospect was getting him down.

He drank his tea unnoticingly – although this matutinal amenity, being a service unprovided by Mrs Lapin, had been pleasing him a good deal.

> *Like a dull actor now,*
> *I have forgot my part, and I am out,*
> *Even to a full disgrace…*

There, once more, was the tiresome Bard running obstinately in his head. But his own business was just to stop being an actor at all – or rather to get back to being one, however unsuccessful and unemployed, in a prosaic and ordinary sense. Only the other day he had read in some column of theatrical gossip in a newspaper that the proposal to take *The Rubbish Dump* to Moscow was believed to have been advanced a further stage. This information had disturbed him; had, indeed, filled him with a very uncomfortable sort of nostalgia. If he hadn't been the prime occasion of that sombre masterpiece's success he had at least received a good deal of favourable notice in it. There was a high probability that if it was really being cast for a foreign tour somebody much more reputable than Mr Norval Falsetto was trying to contact him now. And he had vanished! He had walked out of Mrs Lapin's; he had walked through two hotels; and since then he had never walked again. Gadberry finished his tea, got out of bed, crossed the chilly room, and stared out gloomily over obliterating snows.

Just at the moment – it occurred to him – he couldn't leave Bruton Abbey without leaving an actual physical trail behind him. Miss Bostock would be after him in no time. So, doubtless, would the thwarted and enraged Hon. Alethea, with whole leashes of bloodhounds at her command. Or the Hon. Anthea would send out her St Bernards, bearing little kegs of brandy by which he would be seduced and stupefied. Or Boulter – Gadberry checked himself in this idiotic reverie. Of course it didn't matter two hoots of the Bruton owls what tracks littered the snow. He wasn't in a murder story. Or he wasn't in a murder story *yet*.

He shaved hastily, wondering what had put this last macabre consideration in his mind. It was something that had been said by Miss Bostock, although he couldn't remember just what. Well, he had seen that horrible woman for the last time. Because he *was* bolting. That could be the only explanation of his having had himself called at this early hour. However persuasively Miss Bostock had asserted that he *couldn't* get away; that, as soon as he was unmasked as an impostor, the police would run him down; that he had to stay and play the game out – and more or less as her creature, at that: whatever force there was in all this, he now knew he was going to make a run for it. He was going to be on an express train for the south before the household was tackling its breakfast. He was going to be on Mrs Lapin's doorstep as George Gadberry by the time –

Gadberry broke off in the act of reaching for a suitcase. He mustn't be precipitate. For instance, his position *vis-à-vis* the fiendish Bostock required thinking out. Hadn't there been an element of bluff in her attitude the night before? When he did bolt, would she really set the police on him as an impostor? She'd have nothing to gain by doing so, since as an instrument of getting her claws on the Minton millions he would have become totally written off. And, again, if Boulter's account of her past was true, the police mightn't think highly of her information or assistance. Would she not be inclined simply to call it a day, and sit back on her present employment until some other opportunity of illicit enrichment presented itself?

If this was a correct reading of the situation then he could revert to his former plan. He must contrive to avoid anything in the nature of pursuit or inquiry by taking care to leave Bruton still as the authentic Nicholas Comberford – and as a Nicholas Comberford who had quite outrageously scorned the benefits proposed to be conferred on him. That this would be hard cheese on Aunt Prudence no longer worried him, for his sentiments towards her didn't now get much beyond the plain fact that he disliked her very much. And if he wanted to give offence in a big way, so that his existence would indeed be expunged from the annals of Bruton forever, wasn't the forthcoming grand luncheon party for the Shilbottles a perfect occasion for it?

Rather to his surprise, Gadberry was suddenly aware of a broadly grinning image of himself staring out of the shaving-mirror. It wasn't a beautiful grin – but then beautiful thoughts weren't occasioning it. Perhaps because he had been driven back for so long into a kind of defensive gloom, he found his mind cheerfully rioting in outrage. It was quite wrong to be envisaging with a fiendish glee sundry ways of horrifying Lord and Lady Arthur Shilbottle and their well-built daughters. But it was just this that he continued to do as he dressed. He wouldn't go out with a whimper. He'd go out with a bang.

This proposal (so shocking that the reader ought to be told at once that it was never to fulfil itself) now made Gadberry restless. He had got up at this early hour to no purpose, since there would be plenty of time to pack a bag before the luncheon party. Being thus at a loose end, it suddenly came into his urban mind that it would be rather fun to go out and fool around in the snow. He'd dress himself suitably in knickerbockers, leggings, his deerstalker hat and the like (for he had by now acquired most of the props and costumes of a country gentleman) and walk down to the village and back before breakfast. It might be useful to look at the bus timetable outside the post office. Yes, he'd do that.

Getting out of Bruton Abbey required a certain perseverance and a good memory. After finding the cloisters one had to go through the abbot's arch, the scriptorium, the monks' arch, the strangers' hall and the locutory – by which time one was within sight of the gatehouse. Gadberry achieved all this and finally came to what might quite simply be called the front door. Its large brass handle was being polished by the same young person with whom he had so lately had that abortive encounter in his bedroom. Planning the discomfiture of the Shilbottles had caused his spirits to rise enormously, so this second chance was providential. He grabbed the girl, kissed her handsomely, patted her affectionately on the behind, gave her a straight and honestly admiring look, laughed at her, let her laugh at him, and passed into the open air whistling. He felt happier than he had done for a long time.

It wasn't as cold as he'd expected, and he remembered that one often got a rise in temperature after a heavy fall of snow. He pottered contentedly down the drive, projecting himself for the last time into the role of the young squire, and doing the proper rural things as he went along. He kept himself on the line of the drive without difficulty. The tracks of the Pollocks' car and of Grimble's fly had been almost wiped out by a further fall in the night, but as the drive ran between tremendous beech trees it wasn't possible to go astray. On the lane beyond it was different, but of course it didn't at all matter if he left it; even if he plunged into a deep drift it wasn't likely that he would be struck insensible and perish.

The snow was criss-crossed with tracks of every sort, except that none of them save his own was human. He tried interpreting them as he went along. He had picked up quite a lot of information on such things, partly from the keepers and shepherds and partly from Captain Fortescue; and he found himself thinking that he would be quite sorry not to pick up more. The effect as of a cloven hoof, for example, didn't, as some country-folk liked to believe, proceed from the passing of the Devil himself; it had simply been made by a hare moving fast. And there, going to and fro restlessly along the line of a half-buried hedge, was the track of a fox. But why should it do a kind of nocturnal sentry-go in that fashion? He didn't know. He must ask Fortescue. He had an appointment, he remembered, with Fortescue later that morning. There wouldn't now be much point in keeping it. Perhaps he would, all the same. Fortescue was quite a decent chap; it would be civil in a sense to say goodbye to him, even if it had better be done in not too explicit a manner.

But at the moment he would just drop down into the village of Bruton and then turn back. He was still cheerful, and he applied himself in that spirit to thinking about breakfast. Breakfasts at the Abbey were excellent. After them, he wasn't very clear how he would feel about Mrs Lapin's curiously spurious porridge. But better spurious porridge than a spurious personality, he told himself virtuously. He was whistling again – this time it was a hymn tune – as he walked past the church.

15

So far Gadberry's walk had been through solitude. He hadn't caught sight of another human being, and even the dumb creatures that had left all those tracks in the snow had retired from the scene for the day. There was nothing in sight except the snow itself, and a few drystone dykes half buried in it, with here and there a thorn tree looking as if it had strayed in from a dismal poem of the Romantic period. For some time, too, there hadn't been a sound; silent was the flock in woolly fold, and no audible orisons came from the Reverend Mr Grimble as Gadberry rounded the side of the vicarage. But now this chilly stillness was suddenly shattered by first the throb and then the roar of a fast-moving motorcar. In another moment the vehicle – just to be glimpsed as of a rakishly sporting variety, had swung in from the crossroads at the farther end of the village, and then taken another turn which caused it to disappear among the straggling outbuildings of Mr Grimble's dwelling.

Gadberry judged this to be odd – only mildly so, indeed, but enough to prompt him to take a good look as he walked past. The car had been driven straight into an empty shed, and its driver had closed the door of this, locked it, and proceeded to vanish round a corner before it was possible to get more than a glimpse of him. Gadberry himself walked on. He had gone another dozen yards before becoming aware that the incident had affected him disagreeably.

He couldn't understand why it should be so – except, indeed, that the whole episode gave the impression of having transacted itself with unnatural speed. It was almost possible to believe that the driver of the car had spotted him, and had instantly resolved not to be himself spotted in return. Yes, it was partly that. But it was partly, too, the consequence of a feeling carried over from the previous night. For some quite indefinable reason, the image of the venerable and indeed addle-pated Grimble had become a focus of suspicion in Gadberry's mind. It was his impression that the old person's malignity exceeded even his senility, and that this made him a highly dangerous character. Of course danger was what Gadberry had scarcely ceased looking out for on every quarter since his first rash arrival at Bruton, so that he simply wasn't in a position to view anything or anybody very sanely. Still, the feeling about Grimble was there. What if, quite as much as Miss Bostock, he was a loathsome snake in the grass?

Even as he asked himself this question, Gadberry was aware that he had unconsciously turned round and was now directing his course towards the vicarage. This seemed surprising. When suspecting a snake in the grass one commonly makes rapidly for the high road. But Gadberry's strong sense that he had *had enough* was driving him to a curious rashness. He'd ring Grimble's front-door bell, and go on ringing it until he was admitted, and so had a chance of identifying Grimble's mysterious visitor.

The bell must have been as cracked as its proprietor; it returned a displeasing sound which seemed to traverse empty distances, weave through cobwebs, lose its way in deserted corridors, struggle up or down untrodden staircases. The vicarage was Victorian, dank, gloomy and enormous. Gadberry had no notion under what sort of domestic conditions Grimble inhabited it. But any sort of civilised coping with its brute physical intractability would have required an army of servants that would have put up a tolerable show in the Abbey itself.

Gadberry rang several times. Halfway through this exercise he had a brief impression of somebody peering at him from an upper window. After that nothing at all happened for a long time. Then after that again there came a sound of approaching footsteps – slippered and shuffling footsteps on what must be a bare flagged floor. The front door opened to a cautious crack. The Reverend Mr Grimble was peering out at him.

'Go away,' Grimble said. 'Go away, I say.'

'Good morning, Grimble. It's – '

'I don't give at the door, you know, I don't give at the door.'

'I don't want you to – '

'Charity begins at home, my good man, at home, I say. And that means *your* home, not mine. So go away. Should I choose to visit you in the exercise of my pastoral functions, that will be another matter. It will be another matter, I – '

Wasting no further resource upon idle parley, Gadberry gave the door a long, strong push and walked into the vicarage. With a fine irrationality, Grimble at once shook him cordially by the hand.

'Come in, young man,' he said. 'A matter of the banns of marriage, eh? Well, better to marry than burn, I say. Or rather, *somebody* said – and in a canonical place, if my memory serves. Talking of memory, do you know you remind me of somebody? Young Nicholas Comberford. But you wouldn't know him, my good fellow. He belonged to the gentry. Wipe your boots.'

Not paying much heed to this rubbish, Gadberry glanced curiously around him. So far as he had hitherto thought about Grimble at all, he had imagined him as cared for by some ancient housekeeper as dotty as himself. He saw at once that this couldn't be so. Not the most decrepit rustic crone would suffer such conditions around her. The hall couldn't have been swept through in a twelve-month. The humble lives of rats and mice were much in evidence. There was a bird's nest – a very old one – in the antlers of a stag's head over the bogus Gothic chimney piece. And in the thick dust on the inner surface of a large window a shaky and seemingly impassioned finger had traced:

MARANTHA!

And this – apparently more recently – had been amplified to:

ANATHEMA MARANTHA!

It was painfully clear that the Reverend Mr Grimble, as soon as he stepped within the sanctuary of his vicarage, turned even crazier than he was when on the other side of his doorstep.

'I feel very remiss about never having called on you before,' Gadberry said cheerfully. 'So I thought I'd just look in on passing.' He paused expectantly, but nothing happened. Grimble did, indeed, appear to be listening. But it wasn't to Gadberry. It might have been apprehensively, for some sound he didn't, at the moment, want to be heard. Or it might have been for sign or token audible only to an inner ear. In the gloomy solitude of this hideous house Grimble perhaps beguiled the hours in ghostly conversation – whether with spirits of health or goblins damned. He had obviously been a clergyman for a very long time. Conceivably he had got tired of religion and turned to magic – black magic – instead. Very conceivably that was it. This bizarre notion wasn't a comfortable one, and Gadberry tried to resume his cheery note. 'It's nice,' he said, recalling a frequent conversational resource of Mrs Lapin's, 'to see a little bit of sunshine.'

This, too, wasn't a success. It scarcely deserved to be, since the heavens without remained heavy with unbroken cloud presaging further tremendous snows. And on even a flawless summer day, for that matter, Bruton Vicarage would clearly continue obstinately crepuscular.

'But perhaps I've called at an inconvenient time?' It had come to Gadberry that he had better make a bold plunge. 'I think another visitor has just arrived on you?'

'Another visitor?' The Reverend Mr Grimble was startled. He glanced about him as if in sudden alarm, indeed – and particularly in the direction of an open door on Gadberry's right. Gadberry glanced that way too. What he saw was part of a large and apparently unfurnished room – a dining-room, perhaps, in the blissful nineteenth-century heyday of the Church of England as by law established. It was his first impression that it was now used for the game of badminton, or at least for some pastime involving the laying down of sundry white-painted lines on a bare floor. Perhaps Grimble gathered together the lads and lasses of the village for this blameless diversion as part of what he called his pastoral function. But this didn't seem at all in character with the impression of the old creature that he had now formed. Grimble had every appearance of one who drove his parishioners ferociously from the door.

Gadberry stole another glance. It certainly wasn't *badminton*. There were circles inscribed within triangles, and triangles within circles. Perhaps Grimble went in for *geometry* – and literally in a big way. Gadberry had got no further than this speculation – which wasn't a very bright one – when something happened that was very disturbing indeed. From a point close at hand, and certainly from the interior of the house, a cock crew loudly. The next moment the creature appeared, stalked through the hall, and vanished into the farther room. It was a handsome cock. And it was jet black.

Gadberry turned and stared in horror at the Reverend Mr Grimble. His idle speculation of a few minutes before had been bang in the target area. Magic it was – and black magic at that. This ancient clerk in holy orders was a necromancer!

16

As we have seen, George Gadberry regarded with satisfaction his descent, whether actual or imagined, from that John Gadbury who had been among the most eminent of English astrologers in the seventeenth century. It might be expected, therefore, that he would not be particularly upset upon suddenly finding himself to be in the society of another practitioner of occult arts. But it wasn't so. He was chiefly shocked, no doubt, because of Mr Grimble's regular profession. Gadberry himself, after all, was a vicar's son. He knew that the proper spare-time employment for a rural clergyman, while able-bodied, is to dig in his vegetable garden, weed the drive, chop wood, clean windows, carry coal, and perform similar chores appropriate to his economic standing in the community. When old and feeble, like Mr Grimble, he may get down to a little reading, or to antiquarian research on a local and unassuming basis. But at no time ought he to become a sorcerer.

And it was certainly sorcery to which the black cock pointed. Tonight, or on some night in the near future, the Reverend Mr Grimble, clad in cabbalistic robes and standing within one of those white triangles or circles, would slit the creature's throat, mumbling dark conjurations the while. No wonder the old gentleman was reluctant to admit visitors into his vicarage. If this deplorable vagary became known he would certainly lose his job. Indeed, bishops and archdeacons and their like would be so quick to clamp down on the scandal that they'd have him securely and permanently dumped in the county loony-bin before he could flog the first instalment of his life-story to a Sunday newspaper. And anybody who knew Grimble's secret would decidedly have the whip hand on him.

This last reflection came rather inconsequently into Gadberry's head, and he didn't know why he was momentarily inclined to dwell on it. He certainly had no intention of trying a little blackmail himself as a result of what he'd just discovered. But perhaps –

At this point Gadberry was distracted by a sharp noise from the room into which the cock had strutted. It was the room which he himself had just been able to peer into – the one with the magic formulas, or whatever they were, painted or chalked on the floor. It was a noise suggesting a rash movement on somebody's part, and some object being bumped into or knocked over in consequence. Gadberry decided to investigate. He had pushed rudely into Grimble's hall; he might as well persevere in this course of conduct and push farther. Perhaps the noise had been made by the mysterious visitor. And he now owned a quite irrational anxiety to know who this might be.

Having come to this determination, Gadberry sidestepped Grimble and strode across the hall. Just as he reached the half-open door however, some unseen agency on its other side swung it to. Gadberry grabbed the handle and shoved. The door didn't give. A key must have been turned in it or a bolt pushed home.

'Vexatious,' Grimble said. 'I keep on reporting these matters to the parochial church council. Roof leaks, windows rattle, pipes burst, floors collapse, doors jam. Doors jam, I say. Like this one. You can come into the kitchen.'

'Thank you. I think I'd better be getting back.' If Gadberry's curiosity was still strong, a growing distaste for Grimble and his affairs had suddenly revealed itself as stronger still. And, after all, they *were* Grimble's affairs. That they could in any sense relate to Gadberry's own situation was an idea so irrational that it ought to be discouraged at once. The mysterious stranger, who had nipped so quickly out of his car and into the vicarage, wasn't difficult to explain. Black magic is not commonly an entirely solitary occupation; it is something undertaken by little bands of initiates. No doubt Grimble was joined in his operations by fellow students who had every reason to come and go unremarked. If something was brewing in the near future – eye of newt and toe of frog, for example – there were probably several of these people lurking about the place already. Gadberry decided he didn't want to meet them.

'Quite right, quite right.' Grimble had moved to his front door with surprising nimbleness, and was now flinging it open. 'You mustn't miss your great-aunt's lawyer, eh?' Grimble gave Gadberry a queer look, and suddenly burst into a cackle of shrill laughter. 'Wonderful times ahead, too. Wonderful times ahead, I say. I think they may surprise you. I think they may surprise you very much. Good day to you, Comberford, good day!'

A minute later, Gadberry found himself walking down the overgrown vicarage drive again. It would be an understatement to say that his perturbations had returned. To begin with, it was oddly disturbing to find that Grimble had evidently been quite clear about his identity all along. The business of supposing him to be a parishioner who wanted to get married and so on was entirely bogus. Again, whereas Gadberry would have been prepared to swear that on the previous night Grimble had been only vaguely aware of what was going on, it now appeared that he had been quite on the spot in the matter of Mrs Minton's having announced her testamentary intentions. But that wasn't all. In the final moments of this bizarre encounter the old man had seemed suddenly to lose control of himself. And what had been released, as a conscience, was an obscure and spine-chilling malice. An impression of something of the sort had peeped out of him more than once before. But this time it had suddenly shot up like a jet of venom.

Of course Grimble *was* crazy. For example, his last words had patently carried some sort of ugly and gloating threat. But Grimble seemed not to have been aware of this; he had plainly been supposing himself to be indulging only in the darkest of ironies, invisible except to himself alone. Reflecting on this as he retraced his steps through the snowy solitude, Gadberry discovered in himself a new emotion. An intermittent apprehensiveness and alarm had, in the nature of the case, been familiar to him ever since his arrival at Bruton. But now he felt frightened. And that, somehow, was quite different. He didn't like it at all.

And next he discovered something further. *His sense of sheer fright was giving him a fellow feeling for somebody else.* He was quite sure of this, and yet he was unable to decide in his own mind who the other person could be. Was it Miss Bostock, whose past history and present intentions appeared alike reprehensible? He didn't think it was. Miss Bostock wasn't intimidated. She was intimidating. Was it – But suddenly Gadberry found that he had no further need to speculate. The other frightened character was Grimble himself. That Grimble was frightened was something merely a little obscured by the fact that Grimble was also malevolent.

Hard upon this discovery, Gadberry found his own fright deepening. For a few moments it might even have been described as terror, so that it became his impulse to run for it – literally to run for it – here and now. He'd take to his heels through the snow until he found a railway-station, a bus, a friendly motorist willing to give him a lift – or, all else failing, just a frozen haystack into which he could burrow and hide.

He realised that this was panic. In fact it was quite strictly what used to be called panic in ancient Greece: a conviction that some supernatural power was coming after him. Of course this was nonsense, absolute nonsense. It must have been that damned cock that had done it. He recalled that the bird had affected him with a sense of horror he couldn't account for. Perhaps he'd suffered a traumatic experience with a similar creature in some forgotten woodshed during his childhood.

Trudging doggedly on towards the Abbey – for he commonly discovered in himself some small emergency stock of resolution in extremity – he brought his mind back to Grimble. A mingling of fear and malevolence, he told himself, is precisely what you might expect in one who has dabbled in black magic once too often. It must be the typical emotional state, that was to say, of a man who has yielded to diabolical possession. To have passed wholly within the power of the

Devil must be very frightening. It must also make one, in all one's own impulses, very devilish indeed. That was it. The wretched Grimble was a man constrained by an external power to wickednesses that at once scared and attracted him.

That Gadberry should have come to entertain this highly coloured and Faustian vision of the Vicar of Bruton must appear surprising. Generally speaking, he owned a fairly rational mind. When he departed from the dictates of this – and in the present narrative he has undeniably been discovered as doing so – it was in the direction of behaviour which, if freakish, was yet enterprising and directed to quite reasonable ends: economic security and a recognised place in society. If his course of conduct had been one scarcely to be entered upon by a person of unimpaired moral perception, it had yet not been accompanied by any positive clouding of the intelligence. Yet here he now was, on the verge of believing himself involved in what old magazines would have called a Tale of the Supernatural. Walking towards Mr Grimble's vicarage, he had known very well that certain tracks in the snow had been made by a running hare, and not a prowling Demon. Now he was not so sure.

The Abbey was before him. He stopped and stared at it broodingly. The vast and rambling house, half Gothic and half Gothicised; its peripheral ruins, culminating in a broken and ivied tower which was the chief fastnessm of the Bruton owls; the gardens which were mostly cavernous cypress alleys with here and there a marble statue like a petrified corpse; the fishpond, enormous and mysteriously deep, now frozen over but with here and there a hole driven through the ice for the benefit of the enormous and voracious pike lurking in it: all this must be in part at least responsible for the mediaeval turn which his speculations on Grimble had taken. And of course it was superstitious nonsense, he told himself once more. There must be some other explanation of the puzzle that the old creature presented.

What that explanation could be, Gadberry unfortunately didn't tumble to.

PART THREE

THE PASSING OF NICHOLAS COMBERFORD

17

Gadberry's sole companion at the breakfast-table was Miss Bostock. Fortunately it was the custom at the Abbey that Boulter's principal assistant should be in attendance throughout this meal, and Gadberry was relying upon this to protect him from anything in the nature of renewed full-scale attack. As soon as breakfast was over he'd go out on another prowl, pay his proposed visit to Captain Fortescue, and get back just in time for the luncheon party at which, as Nicholas Comberford, he was going to blot his own copybook – cut his own throat, indeed – gloriously and for ever. Then he'd make his getaway. That Miss Bostock would subsequently denounce him as having been an impostor he continued to think highly doubtful. All the same, he'd do everything his ingenuity could suggest to leave a hopelessly broken trail behind him.

When he entered the breakfast-room, Miss Bostock, who had the air of having been up and about for some time, was accepting a second cup of coffee from the parlourmaid.

'Good morning, Mr Comberford,' she said, and helped herself to sugar.

'Good morning, Miss Bostock. It looks like more snow, wouldn't you say? But at least the gale has dropped. Later on, I hope a little sunshine may break through. We must expect bleak conditions in the next month or so, all the same. The Yorkshire Dales – '

'Quite so.' Miss Bostock had the appearance of proposing to acquiesce amiably in this chatty manner. 'The kidneys are excellent, and this morning I have no criticism of the bacon. You must be hungry after your long tramp.'

'Oh, decidedly.' Gadberry poured thick cream over porridge which wasn't at all like Mrs Lapin's. He gave, in fact, an extra tilt to the jug. He was aware, as he did so, that this was an act of bravado. His appetite wasn't really all that good. He had a suspicion that his inside was proposing to behave as it had been accustomed to do long ago on those three dread mornings in the year when he was due to return to his private school. This terminal phase in the life of Nicholas Comberford was being as nasty as – he supposed – death agonies commonly are.

'How did you find the dear vicar?'

Thus challenged, Gadberry put down his spoon. Since he had taken so much cream, he even put it down with an awkward splash. Was it possible that this ghastly woman had been trailing him? He didn't see how it could have been done – not across all that naked snow.

'Ah, yes,' he said easily. 'I thought I'd just look in on old Grimble, in case last night should have been a bit too much for him. He must have had a chilly drive home. And the vicarage is none too warm and comfortable.'

'No doubt you will be able to do something about that in future years. Evans, I think we shall need a little more toast.'

Evans provided more toast. This, fortunately, didn't involve taking her out of the room. She also stirred the kidneys gently in their sauté dish and dealt expertly with the *filtre à café*. Gadberry watched her gloomily. These high-class ministrations no longer held any charm for him. *Were I from Dunsinane away and clear*, he was telling himself, *Profit again should hardly draw me here*.

'Certainly one's heart bleeds for Mr Grimble's visitor,' Miss Bostock said. 'One can only hope he has brought a hot-water bottle.'

'How on earth can you know –' Gadberry checked himself. Miss Bostock's talk had taken an alarming turn. It looked as if she had spies all over the place. But he himself ought, of course, to remain unperturbed.

'I am a person of some observation, Mr Comberford. You must by this time have remarked the fact. And I am particularly fond of bird watching.'

'Bird watching?' Rather absurdly, Gadberry's mind took a dive in the direction of Grimble's black cock. Perhaps the woman was intimating that she knew about this too.

'The Abbey tower is an admirable station for that sort of thing. Of course the climb is a little hazardous. But I don't mind that. As you know, Mr Comberford, I have fairly strong nerves.'

'Yes, of course.' Gadberry's own nerves were allowing him only to poke rather dubiously at the kidneys which Evans had now placed before him. 'You mean you go up there with binoculars?'

'Quite frequently. And I see what is to be seen. There is a very clear view of the vicarage. Not, of course, that it holds any particular interest for me. Mr Grimble has a hen-run, indeed. But domestic poultry scarcely engage the attention. You will no doubt agree with me there.'

'I suppose so.' Gadberry felt slightly dizzy. The woman *did* know about that black cock.

'Vultures are another matter,' Miss Bostock said.

'*Vultures?*'

'Hawks, of course – yes. I saw several when up on the tower earlier this morning. Local birds of prey are one thing. And they will do well to stick together.' Miss Bostock took a quick glance at Evans, who had moved over to the fireplace to replenish the grate. 'You and I are birds of a feather, are we not?'

'I don't know what you're talking about.' Even as he uttered these words, Gadberry was conscious of their pitifully feeble character. Before he could improve on them, however, Evans was back within hearing again.

'Exotic predators are another matter. Vultures, for example, Mr Comberford. Mr Grimble has his ornithological interests, I think you will agree. But what if he should be harbouring a vulture? You and I might have to tell him he was making a great mistake.'

Gadberry almost repeated 'I don't know what you're talking about'. It would have been a remark at least having the merit of veracity. On the other hand, it would probably be a tactical mistake to admit ignorance at any point where he was not driven to it. So he said nothing at all.

'I have to admit that I am ignorant,' Miss Bostock said – so that Gadberry positively jumped. 'I should like to help dear Mr Grimble to a better ordering of his affairs. I have a notion that he is a little *helpless*. You follow me? It would be well if we could rid him of – well, an *incubus*. Am I right?'

Gadberry had to admit that his breakfast was a shambles. He pushed away his kidneys, half consumed, and groped for a cigarette. An *incubus* was primarily a visitant from a supernatural world. Perhaps this was what Miss Bostock meant. Perhaps she was merely advancing the benevolent thought that the Vicar of Bruton should be disengaged from his injudicious implication with the infernal powers. Or perhaps she was talking about something different. It was already her line that she and Gadberry were fellow conspirators, and that Gadberry would attempt to break away from that only at his peril. Conceivably she had now become aware of some new threat from without, and was proposing that the two of them must close their ranks against this too.

'What is required in bird watching,' Miss Bostock said, 'is patience. But there are times when I feel that rapid results are essential. When this happens, I appeal to fellow students. I admit my ignorance at once. I don't pretend to know what is in fact obscure to me. I say "Tell me what you know, and I will undertake to make sense of it. I will undertake to bring our joint study-project to a successful conclusion."'

'Most interesting,' Gadberry said. He had scrambled to his feet. 'But I must be getting along. I've promised to go across and have a word with Fortescue.'

'I could wish it was fortified with a better breakfast. But perhaps you are saving up for our interesting luncheon.'

'Well, I am rather looking forward to that.' As he said this, Gadberry allowed himself an injudicious grin. Miss Bostock's sharp eyes narrowed on it, and she too got to her feet.

'I hope,' she said, 'that the Shilbottles won't be held up by more snow. Do you know, I think you and I might consult the barometer?'

Gadberry didn't in the least want to consult the barometer. Nor, for that matter, did Miss Bostock. She was merely proposing a course that would take them through the cloisters and out of earshot of Evans. But Gadberry, despite his perception of this, followed her out of the room. It was craven, after all, positively to cower away from the woman.

'By the way, are you a professional actor?' Miss Bostock asked this, casually but suddenly, as soon as they were by themselves. 'It has just come to me that you probably are.'

'I'm not telling you anything about myself. I've said that before.'

'Very well. I was going to inquire if you'd ever played in *Macbeth*. Perhaps as Third Murderer. Anyway, fail not our feast.'

'What do you mean – our feast?' Gadberry very much disliked this riddling talk.

'The luncheon party we were talking of. Go off and see Fortescue, by all means. You're going to have the whole management of the place on your hands, after all. And you won't be wanted for this morning's earlier engagement.'

'Earlier engagement?'

'I sometimes think you're going to be a disastrously stupid confederate. The visit of Mr Middleweek, of course. As you are the principal beneficiary, you can't be called on to act as a witness. I don't know whether I can. But I hope at least to be present. I want to see with my own eyes those dotted lines signed on. The situation is then transformed. We can proceed.'

'Proceed?'

'You certainly are a fool. But about the Shilbottles. You will be civil to both girls indifferently, as the old woman suggested. There isn't any *danger*, you know.' Miss Bostock paused to glance at Gadberry sardonically. 'Long before they can get you in even up to your ankles, the whole thing will be over.'

'It certainly will. I'm going to – '

'You're going to do as you are told. And what you are to be told is extremely simple. It's in *Macbeth* again. *Be bloody, bold, and resolute.* Either that, or leave it to me.'

Gadberry was struck dumb. He could think of nothing to say. Dimly through his head there passed the conjecture that Miss Bostock was as mad as nearly everybody else at Bruton. Perhaps she really saw herself in the character of the Thane of Cawdor's fiend-like Queen. *The raven himself is hoarse… Unsex me here… Make thick my blood…* That sort of thing.

But they had reached the barometer. Miss Bostock – or Lady Macbeth – tapped it briskly and unnoticingly, and walked away.

18

A car drew up at the gatehouse as Gadberry plunged once more into the snow. There could be no doubt about whom it brought to the Abbey. This was Mr Middleweek, Aunt Prudence's solicitor, and in his briefcase were the documents which, in Aunt Prudence's word, were to be executed. The very word itself was somehow sinister. Gadberry had a confused feeling that, once the documents were executed, it mightn't be long before he was executed himself. At least he could no longer pretend that he hadn't a tolerably clear view of what was in the mind of Miss Bostock. When Mrs Minton signed her new will she would at the same time be signing her own death-warrant.

Gadberry of course knew that he wasn't going to kill anybody. He just wouldn't know how to begin. But – he remembered – when Macbeth felt like that, Lady Macbeth showed him just how, and then tidied up the job herself. The result had been to leave Macbeth very awkwardly out on a limb; he'd had to spend the rest of his days wading through blood and so forth in a highly disagreeable manner. It would be the same in his own case. Once Miss Bostock had done the deed (and he had no disposition to believe she wouldn't be perfectly fit for it) he would be helplessly in her hands for keeps. If she was brought to justice he would be brought to justice too. No court would believe that they hadn't been tightly bound together in the planning and carrying out of an ingenious and intricate crime.

He walked on – in the opposite direction, this time, to that which had taken him to the village before breakfast. Captain Fortescue's house lay about two miles away, just beyond the only sizable plantation the landscape boasted. Why he should be continuing to make his way there he just didn't know. His appointment with Fortescue was now meaningless. What he did understand, oddly enough, was precisely what he ought to be doing at this moment. He ought to be retracing his steps to the Abbey. For only one rational course remained to him. It was to make his way instantly into the presence of Mrs Minton and confess to the whole thing. There was quite a chance that she wouldn't prosecute, wouldn't hand him over to the police. Family pride was her ruling passion. She might shrink from exposing that pride to the ridicule that would attend a public exhibition of the manner in which she had been duped. She might simply let him clear out, and then cook up some story to account for his so abruptly vanishing from the Bruton picture.

But Gadberry found that he was walking on. The sunshine for which he had expressed some hopes to Miss Bostock seemed very far from breaking through. The obliterating snows lay everywhere, in some mysterious fashion both dazzling and lustreless, under a sky like a livid lid. He walked for half a mile, and then turned and looked at the Abbey. He had been climbing slightly, and he could now see the River Brut winding its way into the great complex of buildings and then out again. It looked narrower than usual, presumably because it was starting to freeze from its banks inward, and had the appearance of a line scrawled across a virgin sheet of paper by a thick pencil which might have been represented by the Abbey tower. The tower was now a mere stump or stub compared with its former self. It was said to have been the tallest in England, rivalling even the great spires in height. From this point his eye seemed on a level with its crumbled summit. He wondered whether Miss Bostock had returned to her observation-post there, and was at this moment taking advantage of his having turned round to study through her binoculars the expression of consternation which he could feel had settled on his face.

Those proud towers – he found he was saying to himself – *to swift destruction doomed*. The words must be coming to him out of some dreary old poem. And they didn't really apply. For the towers – and there were several, since a fifteenth-century abbot had added one to his lodging, and a nineteenth-century Minton had done the same to the gatehouse – the towers would continue where they were for several further centuries. It was he who was doomed to swift destruction, should he ever return among them. For that, he suddenly realised, was his appalling situation. *He couldn't go back.* His nerve had deserted him. And here he was, a picturesquely fated creature, out in the snow.

To swift destruction doomed. Because his temperament was, after all, theatrical, Gadberry repeated the words to himself with gloomy relish. And the persuasion accompanying them – that he simply could not set foot in Bruton Abbey again – ought to have passed in a matter of seconds or minutes. It ought to have represented no more than another quick flare-up of panic, which would depart leaving him harassed indeed but not helpless. Only this time it didn't seem to be working that way. There had suddenly come upon him a settled conviction that he could *not* return to the ghastly mess that he had contrived for himself.

He had about fifteen pounds in his pockets. He was dressed in clothes which, although new, expensive, and congruous with the rural solitudes through which he was at present moving, would look not quite right on Mrs Lapin's doorstep. He had nowhere any other possessions in the world – except behind him in the Abbey, where he had probably been signed up as heir to the whole place within the last ten minutes. *In vain, in vain*, he told himself. He recalled with astonishment his light-hearted plan to quit after some episode of freakish clowning at the expense of the innocuous if no doubt boring Shilbottles. Between him and any such nonsense there now lay the grim shadow of Mrs Minton's fiend-like companion.

Three miles beyond Fortescue's house ran the high road. If he trudged on there he might pick up a lift that would take him quite a long way – even into Leeds, a comfortingly large and anonymous sort of city. There he could take breath and think, before presumably spending an uncomfortably appreciable part of that fifteen pounds on a second-class railway ticket to London.

So Gadberry trudged on. There wasn't another moving creature in sight. In a field on his right, indeed, quite a lot of sheep had for some reason been left to make what they could of their cheerless environment. But the sheep simply stayed put. They seemed entirely contented. Every now and then they made noises expressive of nothing in particular. Gadberry envied them their humble lot.

He had come to a point at which the dale rose in a short swell on his left, dipped to an invisible hollow, and then rose again steeply to a considerable height. On this latter surface the snow was marked with a vaguely familiar species of zigzag lines. He glanced at these without interest, and hurried on. It was starting to snow again: first in large, spectacular flakes which would have looked well on a Christmas card, and then in very small ones which plainly meant business. He turned up his collar. It was while he was in the act of doing this that he heard a cry.

'*Help! Oh, please, help!*'

Gadberry stopped in his tracks. What was astonishing was not the suddenness of the appeal, but the thing done to him by an indefinable quality in the appealing voice. Had he paused to think, he might have said that the Vale profound was overflowing with the sound, or that a voice so thrilling ne'er was heard in spring-time from the Cuckoo-bird. As it was, he scrambled over the snow-covered dyke beside him without pausing for a moment. The voice had been a girl's, and it had instantly declared itself as of magical beauty. Gadberry plunged towards it like a man whose fate has caught up with him.

Philosophically regarded, there can be little doubt that what had taken place was an event of considerable psychological complexity. It will be recalled that Gadberry was a young man markedly susceptible to female charm, but that by constitution he was one fondly overcome by this intermittently and violently rather than in a settled and diurnal manner. A frolic such as he had indulged in that morning with the little housemaid was really something to which he had, so to speak, to address his mind; it was more or less the right thing to be doing as a regular part of what one owed to being alive and healthy and twenty-seven years old. But this catastrophic business was another matter, and it came along rarely. That it had come along now was partly the consequence (as in the next thirty seconds he was overwhelmingly to see) of a single absolutely objective fact. But it undoubtedly had an origin, too, in his own present depressed and disordered situation. For a long time he had been hearing nothing but voices that were either boring or disagreeable or ominous or downright threatening. And now, suddenly, there was this.

The girl lay in a flurry of snow and a glory of golden hair. His first impulse was to look away from her, quite dazzled – so it was from the fur hat which had tumbled from her head that he first realised she was no country wench. Nor do country wenches dress in anoraks above – or, below, in slacks tailored with an inspiration to make the head swim. And they don't, for that matter, lie around in a tangle of skis.

'Oh, thank goodness!' The girl got this out with a gasp, so that he realised like a stab of pain that she was in pain herself. He knelt down beside her. But, as he did so, his glance went to the ski-tracks on the slope above.

'You ought to have the kind that flick off when you tumble,' he said. 'They're much the best for beginners.' He spoke almost roughly – which made it surprising that he had simply gathered the girl in his arms. 'And it was stupid, anyway. The snow's all wrong.'

'That's what Daddy said. But I did so want to practise. I'm going to Switzerland next week. It's terribly kind of you to help me.' The girl moved in Gadberry's grasp, but it wasn't precisely a movement of disengagement. 'I'm afraid my ankle hurts rather. Had I better try to stand up?'

'We must get the skis off first. Which ankle is it?'

'It's…it's the left. Always been a bit wobbly since my pony did a roll on it…*ow!*'

'I'm frightfully sorry. I'll be terribly careful.' To his horror, Gadberry found that he had been fumbling at one of the skis while still unable to take his gaze from the girl's face. She was the most radiantly beautiful person he had ever seen.

'Isn't it sickening?' the girl said. 'What if I can't go? To Switzerland, I mean. Of course, I've only been home for a week. But life's so boring here. I say – do you mind my asking? Are you by any chance Mr Comberford?'

'Yes, I am.' So strangely are we formed that Gadberry gave this reply without the slightest consciousness of duplicity. In this situation, somehow, he *was* Nicholas Comberford. 'Who are you?'

'Evadne. Evadne Fortescue.'

Although Gadberry had lately judging both Alethea and Anthea to be absurd and affected names, he now had no such impression about Evadne. It was a lovely name in itself. And the cadence it formed with 'Fortescue' was exquisite.

'There's a tremendous girl in an Elizabethan play called Evadne,' he said. 'I once – ' Oddly enough, although now again Nicholas Comberford, he was about to say 'I once acted in it'. But he checked himself in time. 'I once knew another Evadne,' he said. 'But she wasn't remotely as beautiful as you are.'

Although still in evident pain, Miss Fortescue laughed. She also blushed – or at least Gadberry persuaded himself that she did so. And now she did draw away.

'Thank you,' she said. 'But don't be absurd, all the same, Mr Comberford. And now I must manage to get home. It's not very far. I'm sure I can hobble.'

'I'll come with you, of course. In fact, I'm on my way to call on your father now.'

'How very odd!'

'Odd?' Gadberry was puzzled.

'The coincidence, I mean. That you should be coming to see Daddy, and that I should take a tumble like this, pretty well straight in your path.'

'Well, yes – I suppose so.' Gadberry had got the skis off, and was now laying them down on the snow. 'We'll have to abandon these for the time being. Now then' – and he stooped over Evadne Fortescue – 'here goes.'

126

'What do you mean?'

'I'm going to carry you, of course. It's no distance.'

'But you can't possibly! I'm frightfully heavy. In fact I'm most disgustingly fat.' Miss Fortescue paused. 'You'll see,' she added.

'There!' Gadberry had swung her up into his arms. As he had expected, she was neither too heavy nor too light. At every point, so to speak, there was precisely as much of her as there ought to be. Not that he made this calculation in any carnal spirit. On the contrary, a kind of blazing innocence surrounded his instantaneous and utterly fateful relationship with this divinity. He suddenly remembered the childish episode of that morning, when he had hugged, kissed and playfully smacked the little housemaid. He laughed aloud at its complete absurdity.

'What are you laughing at?' The ravishing Evadne, although nestled in his arms, spoke suspiciously. 'I suppose you think I've been an absolute idiot...ow!' She had winced and exclaimed as Gadberry took a first cautious forward step. 'It *does* rather hurt. I expect it will have to be set, or something.'

'I'm sure they'll put it right in no time. And I'll try to go frightfully carefully.'

'Can you really manage? You must be terribly strong.'

Gadberry laughed again. His face was very close to Evadne's. And his muscles were, in fact, in very good trim. He was naturally quite a stalwart as well as a personable young man, and a country life had been adding agreeably to these graces. Really and truly, he wasn't a bad match for Evadne Fortescue. He felt very happy. So, presumably, did Evadne, for she now let her head drop on his shoulder with a gentle sigh. She might almost have been passing into a mild swoon.

'I'm terribly lucky to have found you,' she murmured. 'It's been like meeting a knight-errant. You know? Sir Galahad, or somebody like that.'

Sir Galahad Gadberry... With infinite care – because his head was swimming a little – Gadberry lifted his precious burden over the

dyke. Then he bore her triumphantly through the thickly falling
snow.

19

The Misses Shilbottle – Hon. Alethea and Hon. Anthea – were very nice girls. Perhaps it would have been more logical to say that they were a very nice girl, since one was quite as indistinguishable from the other as the diabolical Miss Bostock had averred. Breadth of pelvis was perhaps their most striking feature; if you were simply concerned to embark on steady breeding in a no-trouble way then a Shilbottle would be a tiptop buy. In addition to large, frank, wholesome bodies they had large, frank, wholesome laughs. They talked about hunting (to Mrs Minton's disapproval) and hunt balls, about beagles, about harriers, about point-to-points, about the pursuit of otters, about the shooting of pheasants, partridges and grouse, about the extricating of trout, salmon and other fishes from the flood. Some centuries ago – Gadberry reflected – they would have talked about bear-baiting or badger-baiting or cock-fighting in the same jolly way. They weren't Gadberry's idea of a bedfellow any more than the tweedy and bony Lord and Lady Arthur were his idea of parents-in-law. But he was delighted with them, all the same. The plain fact that they were resolved to have a shot at the heir of Bruton, and severally to accept triumph and defeat in a sporting family spirit – with perhaps, he dimly felt, a flyer staked on the result: this didn't disconcert him in the least. Indeed, he was quite prepared to adore them, since all women ought to be adored. And he hadn't, needless to say, the slightest difficulty in dividing his favours equally and courteously between them, any more than he had difficulty in listening respectfully to their father, or offering their mother the sort of deference proper to an American heiress who has married a marquis' younger son.

Mrs Minton – who hadn't, of course, a glimmer that her supposititious great-nephew was deliriously and transformingly in love – evinced high gratification at the success of her luncheon party. Miss Bostock – although her eyes did occasionally narrow consideringly on the spectacle – couldn't have anything to complain of. Boulter poured wine at his young master's direction, and murmured confidentially into his young master's ear, and passed trifle (for it was trifle again) very much as if it were already the wedding cake. It was, Gadberry judged, a happy, happy party all round.

For the time being, in fact, Sir Galahad was on top. Gadberry's strength was as the strength of ten because his heart was pure. An honourable and elevating passion had taken entire command of him. Everything else would sort itself out.

He ought, of course, to have been abashed. Alethea and Anthea were girls of practical instinct and realistic mind. But he could see that they weren't mercenary in anything that could be called a corrupt way. The proposed transaction (as it might be called) had a basis in the implicit assumption that he was himself out of the right stable. He could be trusted without inquiry to measure up to the required reliabilities and decencies and loyalties. Once that was clear, you went ahead in a sensible, open and (for that matter) simply animal way. It wasn't a very exalted code, but it was a perfectly healthy one. And it was how Shilbottles produced Shilbottles, generation by generation. Yes, he ought to be abashed that, as well as being raised immeasurably above it by reason of his new and ennobling passion, he was also depressed a damnably long way below it through the shocking wickedness of his being at Bruton at all. But at present nothing of all this existed at all notably in Gadberry's head. He was fathom-deep in the euphoria – which is also the cruel madness – of love.

He hadn't as yet at all taken in the extent of the revolution in his own feelings and attitudes. For example, he had walked back to the Abbey from the Fortescues' house without its once having come clearly into his head that this was a route he had determined never to take again. Since to leave Bruton was now unthinkable, he just didn't think about it at all. Or at least he had dropped the problem into cold storage after giving it no more than the briefest reappraisal in his mind. Miss Bostock – and she was really rather an absurd and melodramatic character – was the nub of the matter so far as any actual urgency went. And even supposing that she was veritably Lady Macbeth to the life (or death) it was still not to be supposed that she was planning to act with anything like the breathtaking speed with which events had moved in that castle at Inverness. Mrs Minton's new will, together with whatever related documents were involved, had of course been signed by this time. But it could hardly be Miss Bostock's intention, within hours or even days of this, to lure her employer into (say) a little bird watching from the top of the Abbey tower and then briskly tumble her over the edge. That would be to give altogether too rum an appearance to the whole affair. A substantial breathing space, therefore, there must necessarily be.

Meantime, Gadberry had better things to think about. He had, that is to say, Evadne Fortescue to think about – and so much was he keyed up by the amazing events of the morning that he found himself able to engage in this intoxicating pursuit almost uninterruptedly even while he was being, to all appearances, perfectly attentive to Mrs Minton's guests.

One small cloud did hang over his contemplations. He had from the first regarded Aunt Prudence's agent, Captain Fortescue, as a very decent sort of chap. But this had been a matter of business relations and casual social encounters. Now, he had seen Fortescue for the first time in his paternal character, and he wasn't at all sure that the man was adequate in the role. Or at least, although he might have been an adequate parent in a general way, it didn't seem at all certain that he was adequate to being the parent of Evadne.

The Fortescue household, he had found, consisted only of Evadne, a younger brother whom he had judged insufficiently appreciative of the privilege of owning such a sister, and Captain Fortescue himself. Fortescue, it seemed, was a widower of many years standing. In such a position it must be quite a job bringing up a daughter, and perhaps one would come to feel the necessity of guarding against too much fondness. Perhaps this was why Fortescue had appeared a little cool towards his darling child when Gadberry had marched into the house and planted her with infinite gentleness on the drawing-room sofa. He had even – come to think of it – appeared embarrassed, and had been in more of a hurry to find Gadberry a drink than to determine the extent of his daughter's injury. When Gadberry had insisted on ringing up Dr Pollock at once, Fortescue had rather oddly temporised. And Evadne herself, indeed, had followed his lead, although she was obviously in the most awful pain. Was she – Gadberry wondered – bullied by her father? His blood ran first cold, and then hot, at the thought. But at least Pollock had finally been summoned – although Gadberry had been surprised to hear Fortescue tell him that he needn't hurry over before lunch.

The recollection of this seeming callousness was a little disturbing Gadberry now. Fortunately he was able to assure himself that it was, at the most, only one side of the picture. Perhaps Fortescue, as an old military man, believed in stiff upper lips and so forth when it came to minor injuries. Certainly he was an *admiring* parent. Gadberry had seen enough to be in no doubt about that. It was precisely a kind of reluctant admiration that Fortescue could several times be observed as directing upon his daughter. Again, when Gadberry had taken his leave, Fortescue had accompanied him silently some way down his drive. Several times he had appeared prompted to speak, but he had not in fact got round to doing so. Something like embarrassment had again overtaken him. Probably he had been wanting to tell Gadberry what a marvellous girl Evadne was, and then shyness had prevented him. Finally he had shaken hands, still in silence, and with a look which, deprived of its context, one might have taken for an odd sort of compunction. But that didn't make sense. He must have realised the instantaneous and powerful nature of the passion which this young man had conceived for his adorable daughter, and been in fact commiserating with Gadberry on having to leave his beloved, even for a short space of time, in discomfort and even pain.

Thus did Gadberry meditate, even while listening attentively to Shirley Shilbottle – otherwise Lady Arthur – while she entered with some particularity into the history of her family. For generations its ladies appeared to have made quite a thing of conferring their hands and fortunes upon titled persons all over Europe. It seemed a harmless and indeed benevolent form of dedication, and Gadberry made all the appropriate responses. But he was really wondering, of course, about when he could next see Evadne. It would be perfectly proper to call at the Fortescues again that afternoon, but only perhaps to make polite inquiries about the sufferer at the door. He had discovered in himself, in her, in their relationship, a rare – and at first perhaps a fragile – thing. It was like a bud that he must now devote his whole energy to coaxing into flower. Apart from this, nothing else mattered. Undeniably, of course, there were awkwardnesses. Equally undeniably, some of them were in that moral sphere in which it was so hard not to feel a certain perplexity. But, somehow or other, it would all straighten itself out. Mrs Minton, for instance, couldn't but acknowledge the transcendent worth of Evadne Fortescue as soon as it was brought within her purview. She might well be so enchanted by his capture of such a prize (when he *did* capture it) that she would be very willing to overlook the slightly irregular manner in which he had become her heir – supposing the worst came to the worst and she ever had to know about it.

Gadberry, sunk in his madness, took the Shilbottle girls on a little after-luncheon conducted tour of Bruton. He continued to apportion his attention scrupulously between them. His thoughts were far away. But he was aware that they were both, poor dears, deciding that Yes, he'd do.

20

When Gadberry came down to breakfast next morning he found to his relief that Miss Bostock had finished her meal and departed. As Mrs Minton invariably breakfasted in her own room this meant that Gadberry was able to begin the day delightfully with one sole companion. Needless to say, this wasn't the parlourmaid. It was the divine image of Evadne herself. He planted this invisible presence firmly before him on the other side of the table, and communed with it rapturously while eating everything he could lay his hands on.

So absorbed was he in this agreeable reverie that it was some time before he noticed that the parlourmaid wasn't there anyway. He was being waited on by Boulter in person. This was unusual. Presently, however, he decided that it was also satisfactory in itself. He had a wholesome longing to communicate to some other living creature at least some shadow of his bliss. The parlourmaid wouldn't here have been a practical proposition. But with Boulter a little familiar conversation was entirely in order. If only very cautiously, he could skirt the sole topic which alone lay close to his heart.

'I liked those Shilbottle girls very much,' he began. 'They struck me as good sorts.'

'Precisely so, sir. I am in agreement with you. Although, indeed, "decent fellows" is the expression that would spring to my own lips. There is something a little masculine, to my mind, about that vigorously outdoor type.'

'That's perfectly true.' Over his raised coffee cup, Gadberry glanced at Boulter in surprise. It had occurred to him before that there was something rather deep about Boulter. Perhaps – he thought, with a twinge of uneasiness amid his new-found joy – something a little too deep. Still, he seemed a sensible man. 'But Mrs Minton has a high opinion of them,' he went on. 'Of both of them. Or, one might say, of either equally.'

'Quite so, sir. I am aware that the mistress has her plans.'

'She damned well has.' Caution ought to have shut Gadberry up at this point. So should propriety, since offering to Boulter such an expression about his employer was to put him in a false position. But it was very evident that Boulter could look after himself. 'Of course,' Gadberry went on, 'one has to admit it's a rational notion. Healthy girls who would produce healthy kids. Adjoining estates. A considerable fortune. Same class of society, and all that stuff. But a chap ought to be allowed his own say in a matter of that sort, if you ask me.'

'Yes, sir. Yes, indeed. Anything to the contrary is quite unusual in the modern age.'

'But the trouble is that the old lady may be dead set on it. And, of course, she might…well, totally change her mind about me still at any time.'

'I judge not, sir.'

'What on earth do you mean?'

'Well, sir, it is a matter of great confidence. Nevertheless it will be proper, no doubt, that I should put you in possession of certain relevant facts. Perhaps I should mention that the will of the late Mr Minton made provision for the pensioning of such upper servants as should be in the employment of the household at the time of his widow's decease, or should pass out of that employment after a certain term of service during her remaining lifetime. Such arrangements are quite common, I understand, among persons of property. A special fund is constituted for the purpose. The effect is a little to mitigate the oppressive incidence of certain current trends in social legislation.'

'Death duties and things, you mean?' There was something a shade overpowering, Gadberry found, in Boulter's notion of a chatty English prose.

'Indeed, yes. And I mention these matters only to explain how it came about that I was in a position to be called in as a witness to the dispositions made by Mrs Minton yesterday. No interest of my own was involved.'

'I see. And you got a look at what it was all about?'

'At a modicum of it, sir, at a modicum. There was one instrument which it was not very clear to me that Mrs Minton fully understood. It concerned an irrevocable trust, and its effect has been to take a very considerable part of the properties involved out of Mrs Minton's control and vest them in trustees. The trustees are professional people: bankers, solicitors and accountants. And they are now under a legal obligation to execute their trust in a manner which, according to their independent judgment, is in the best interest of the beneficiary – who is of course yourself. They *could* consult Mrs Minton in any matter. But they would be challengeable if it in any way appeared that they were acting in a manner suggested or dictated by a whim of hers.'

'You mean she's made me more or less independent here and now – and without knowing it?'

'Well, sir, I have not been trained to the law. But the position is at least an interesting one. And there is a thought in that, sir. There is distinctly a thought in it.'

'She *is* in a bit of a muddle about it.' Gadberry was staring in a kind of awe at the efficient Boulter. 'And so is Miss Bostock.'

'Miss Bostock, sir?' Boulter spoke rather sharply.

'She was there a couple of nights ago, when Mrs Minton was explaining her intentions. We both got the impression that all this signing of documents and so forth was going to affect matters only after Mrs Minton's death.'

'In my judgment, sir, that remains true in relation to the greater part of the property. At the same time, there is this matter of the trust to which I have referred. Were you and Mrs Minton to fall out, it would appear to me very doubtful whether you could, in the old phrase, be cut off with a penny.'

'If we fell out over this marriage business, for instance?'

'An excellent example to take, sir. Were you yourself to propose a perfectly suitable marriage, and Mrs Minton to attempt to insist on another, it would be very difficult for the trustees to give her their support.'

'I see. It takes a bit of thinking about, doesn't it?'

'Exactly, sir. It is, as I said, a thought.'

Gadberry finished his coffee – which he had neglected to do during this absorbing conversation – and fell momentarily into a muse. When he emerged from it, it might have been said that Sir Galahad was in control again. It had been, after all, one of the prime tenets of chivalry that a lady's eyes, favourably bent upon a knight, could inspire him to fight like mad. Gadberry had more than a hope that Evadne Fortescue's eyes were bent precisely that way upon him. So it was jolly well his business to stand in his tracks and fight it out. He was shocked to think that, a mere twenty-four hours previously, he had been planning a craven flight from Bruton Abbey.

Moreover – and with that marked clarity of vision which sexual infatuation brings – he was now seeing his way much more confidently through those ethical intricacies of his situation which had from time to time obscurely troubled him in the past. Mrs Minton *ought* to have an heir, since her wish so to be provided was blameless and indeed laudable. On the other hand a sound morality was far from requiring that the real Nicholas Comberford should necessarily take on the job. If he had other ideas, that was his own affair. And if he chose to provide a substitute, thus gratifying his great-aunt's wish and at the same time securing a suitable provision both for himself and for a well-qualified understudy (so to speak) or stand-in, the result was plainly advantageous to all concerned.

Gadberry was naturally delighted that the mists had once more parted before him in this way, and the simplicities of the matter been restored to him. And now, moreover, there was an additional factor conducing to the absolute rightness of what he was in course of achieving. There was Evadne. Evadne was going to make him the happiest of mortals, and he was going to do his best to carry out the

137

same job by her. It was clear that anything – even if it were a mild deception – calculated so immensely to enhance the stock of the world's bliss must be absolutely right in itself.

Thus heartened, Gadberry resumed his colloquy with the impassive Boulter.

'As a matter of fact,' he said fondly, 'there is another girl. I dare say you know her. Captain Fortescue's daughter. Miss Evadne.'

'Ah, yes indeed, sir. Although she has not been much in these parts of recent years, I have occasionally seen her at divine service. If I may presume, sir, I would wish to congratulate you on your taste.'

'Thank you very much.' Boulter, Gadberry thought, although a shade stiff in his manner, was undoubtedly a very good fellow.

'A great beauty, sir. A toast, as the gentlemen used to say. Decidedly a toast. It must certainly be arranged, sir. The romance, if I may term it, must be facilitated. I am decidedly with you in that.'

'I'm very glad to hear it.' Gadberry was naturally delighted at thus so readily securing Boulter as an ally.

'A high degree of satisfaction in that sphere, sir, conduces remarkably to a young gentleman's content. At least for several years, sir. It depends, of course, upon the temperaments involved. Later on, congruous tastes and habits – what is sometimes called compatibility of temperament – come increasingly into play.'

'I suppose so.' Gadberry wasn't sure that there was any occasion for Boulter's launching out on this homiletic vein.

'But at the start, one must agree, the sensual music is the thing. I draw the expression, sir, from a poem by the late Mr Yeats.'

'Yes, of course.' This time, Gadberry gazed at Aunt Prudence's extraordinary butler in positive alarm.

'When the rites of marriage go well, a young gentleman is likely to be the more amenable in other fields. He will not stand strictly upon terms.'

'Boulter, what on earth are you talking about?'

'It may be, sir, that your continued residence at the Abbey will require that certain compromises – chiefly of a financial nature – will have to be made. Should you be securely in the enjoyment of the riches of the marriage-bed, you will be the less sticky about paying up.'

'About paying up?' It was perhaps Boulter's abrupt descent to normal colloquial expression that chiefly startled Gadberry now. Then he thought he understood. 'My God!' he said. 'Do you mean that ghastly woman?'

Very respectfully, Boulter removed Gadberry's empty coffee cup from beneath his nose, and began clearing the table. Gadberry watched him in silence. He was now puzzled and disturbed – but it had been rash, all the same, to come out with that last question. In the nature of the case, the dire problem of Miss Bostock must remain private and his own. He had no doubt – such is the fortifying power of love – that he would solve it effectively enough. Perhaps – it suddenly and surprisingly came to him – *she* could just be tipped off the top of the Abbey tower. Such a solution would be, in her own phrase, extremely simple and elegant. Or alternatively – But Boulter had resumed his discourse. Gadberry's exclamation didn't seem to have surprised him at all.

'I take it, sir, that you refer to Miss Bostock. I did not, in point of fact, have her in mind. But she certainly brings up a relevant consideration. Decidedly so. The other evening, as I think you will recall, you and I were in agreement that she is a dangerous woman. It is a fact that is the more apparent to me now.'

'The more apparent? What do you mean?'

'She is an observant woman. It is a faculty, sir, which I think I may claim to share with her. I am myself, as another of our poets has it, a man who notices things. And Miss Bostock is a woman who notices things. We are, perhaps, evenly matched. That is why, sir, I hope to be of assistance to you. On mutually advantageous terms.'

'Boulter, I haven't the least idea what you are – '

'Come, come, sir – if I may use the expression without impertinence. It is very apparent to me that Miss Bostock has most unfortunately arrived at the truth.'

'The truth?'

'She knows – does she not? – that you are an impostor. You will pardon the expression, sir.'

'Look here –'

'Let us not bandy words, sir.' Boulter remained wholly impassive. 'Let us rather reconstitute our relationship, sensibly and profitably, in terms of the facts of the case. You are not Mr Nicholas Comberford.'

21

Boulter must be pushed off the top of the tower too. Prowling the gardens between snow showers after he had got away from the man, Gadberry arrived at this rational conclusion readily enough. And it wouldn't do to arrange, so to speak, successive precipitations. Boulter must go, Miss Bostock must go, and Mrs Minton had better go as well. But it must all happen at once. A bird-watching party was conceivable. Mrs Minton and her companion should be lured up the tower in this ornithological interest, and then Boulter should be instructed to take them up, say, plum cake and Madeira. And then – ? Well, one could have buried in the mouldering structure a small charge of dynamite. It would be perfectly decent to get married a month or thereabouts after the triple funeral.

Gadberry circumambulated the fishpond. He even advanced cautiously over the ice – it was now very thick – and peered into one of the large, jagged holes that had been smashed in it for the benefit of the pike. He had on several occasions just glimpsed these celebrated creatures. They were enormous. Nowhere in England were there pike like the Bruton pike. They devoured perch by the ton. If you were to fall in and drown – an ancient gardener had assured Gadberry – they would have picked you to whispers before your corpse developed any of those distressing qualities which would bring it to the surface again. In the old days the pike had accounted for several lay brethren who, as a consequence of monastic inebriety, had mistaken the smooth surface of the fishpond in the moonlight for the smooth surface of the bowling green under the same treacherous illuminant.

As for Abbot Jocelin, he had simply been pitched to the ravening brutes during the celebrated revolt of the children of the singing school in the year – Gadberry seemed to remember – 1423.

> *How tedious is a guilty conscience!*
> *When I look into the fish-ponds in my garden,*
> *Methinks I see a thing armed with a rake,*
> *That seems to strike at me…*

The Cardinal in *The Duchess of Malfi* was, of course, mad. Gadberry, with the Cardinal's celebrated meditation thus floating into his head, realised that he was quite capable of going mad himself. Merely to harbour a fantastic vision of liquidating his embarrassments with high explosive was to be pretty mad. Still, he wasn't beyond recalling himself to sanity here and now. What he had to do was to work out a rational programme in the light of the latest change in his situation.

It was, of course, very disconcerting that Boulter, as well as Miss Bostock, *knew*. And didn't – he had almost forgotten him – the Reverend Mr Grimble show signs of at least some glimmering of the same awareness? This really left only Mrs Minton herself. What if *she* knew, and was for some fiendish reason dissimulating her knowledge? Gadberry's head swam. He stepped back in nervous haste from that sinister aperture in the ice.

That both Miss Bostock and Boulter *knew* affected, in the first place, simply what might be called the pay-out. They wanted Gadberry securely established as the heir of Bruton because they wanted their whack. But the female of the species was more deadly than the male. Compared with Miss Bostock, whose fell purpose no compunctious visitings of nature were going to touch, Boulter positively dripped the milk of human kindness. He seemed perfectly prepared to continue to put up with Mrs Minton in the land of the living if only her supposed great-nephew and, as a consequence, her butler, were to enter substantially into the enjoyment of the Bruton revenues at an early date.

Both these people, Gadberry had to admit, had the spurious Nicholas Comberford under their thumb. So had the authentic Nicholas Comberford – who clearly couldn't be ignored just because he was rather mysteriously quiescent at the moment. Of whatever came in, Comberford was to have a half. And there would be Boulter and Miss Bostock to satisfy after that. It was a prospect that didn't seem too good. Yet it had its brighter side. Any of the three could give him away. But all three would pretty certainly take themselves off the payroll if they did so. Comberford, as the originator of the deception, could expect no favour from his outraged great-aunt, and he would probably go to jail into the bargain. Boulter and Miss Bostock, if they were clever at putting nothing on the record, might possibly elude the law. But a showdown would automatically kill the goose that laid their golden eggs. Gadberry himself had only to keep his nerve in order to ensure that – the true Comberford apart – he had no more than two minor pensioners on his hands.

And, once more, there was no absolute urgency about the affair. Boulter's was a waiting game, and two could play at that. Miss Bostock, it was true, intended nothing less than murder as soon as it should be convenient. He was quite clear about this. But convenience, as he had already reassured himself, required the passing of some decent interval of time. It required, too, the rigging of something that was to have the appearance of natural death. Mrs Minton was going to be murdered. But her death was never to be *seen* as that. And to contrive the appearance either of accident or fatal illness was to require at least a little thinking out. Tonight, tomorrow, the next day: to organise his own plans and defences he had at least as much breathing space as that.

Gadberry's brow cleared a little as he worked this out. That there could be any fallacy in so simple a chain of reasoning never entered his head.

Boulter was waiting for him in the cloisters. The man's bearing was monumentally respectful. Perhaps he was just being cautious, since any curious fellow servant could successfully eavesdrop in this murky place. More probably he was proposing to get a perverse enjoyment from continuing to behave in this way.

'Mrs Minton's compliments, sir. She proposes to pay a call on Lady Arthur Shilbottle this afternoon, and will be glad to know that you are able to drive her over.'

'Oh, bother!' Although merely amused that Aunt Prudence was thus proposing to force the pace, Gadberry didn't at all welcome the idea of having to spend his afternoon in such an expedition. He had, needless to say, planned an expedition of his own. He was going to walk over and see Evadne. She would probably be in bed, but perhaps she would only be immobilised on a sofa. In either case, he intended to see her. If there was any difficulty about going in and kneeling at her bedside, he would obviate it by making a firm declaration of his suit to her father first. After that, and despite all the lover's diffidence that he could summon, he was confident that he could gain her troth pretty well by storm. For it was his instinct that it had been love at first sight with her, just as it had been with him. Through all her maidenly modesty, through all her sweet confusion upon their utterly unexpected encounter, her eyes, somehow, had declared it. And now there was going to be delay because of this stupid plan.

'Is that the message you would wish me to convey, sir?'

'The message?'

' "Oh, bother", sir. You would wish me to tell Mrs Minton that?'

'Don't be a fool, Boulter. You know we must go easy with her. Say I'll be delighted. And find something I can take to those tiresome young women. As a present, I mean. No harm in playing up a bit.'

'Quite so, sir. What sort of object would you have in mind?'

'I haven't the slightest idea. A puppy, perhaps.'

'I judge it improbable, sir, that anything of the sort is available just at the moment. Or not of a suitably thoroughbred variety. There might possibly be a kitten.'

'Very well – a kitten. Or a canary or some furry caterpillars.'

'Thank you, sir. I will see what can be done.'

Gadberry walked away impatiently. It just wasn't possible to perturb Boulter. And now, he supposed, his best plan would be to try to speak to Evadne on the telephone. In one way or another he must ceaselessly show his devotion to the dear girl. To let a whole day pass without some manifestation of it was inconceivable.

He made his way, therefore, to the instrument. It stood in the locutorium, and so wasn't as privately placed as he would have liked, but he must risk that. He got through, and was answered by Captain Fortescue.

'Fortescue? This is Comberford speaking.'

'Ah, good morning. I was thinking we ought to have another word soon. To tell the truth, Comberford, I'm not happy. Not happy at all.'

'I'm sorry about that.' Gadberry felt distinctly dashed.

'About the new tenant at Stonesfield. Are you?'

'As a matter of fact, I'm not thinking about – '

'Perhaps I'd better run over and get your instructions. Is that what you have in mind?'

'No, it isn't. Not in the least. I've rung up to ask about Evadne. How is she?'

'Evadne? Very well, thank you. Or rather, in considerable pain still. She'll have to lie up for some days. Good of you to inquire. Goodbye.'

'Fortescue – hold on!' There was an agitation in the voice coming over the wire which puzzled Gadberry a good deal. 'The fact is, I want to – ' Now Gadberry in his turn was agitated. 'Look here, can I speak to her?'

'Yes, of course. I mean, no. That's to say, she's been told she mustn't try to get on her feet. Better not bring her to the telephone.'

'Of course not.' Gadberry felt ashamed of his thoughtlessness. 'Will you just tell her I meant to come over and see her this afternoon, but now I find I have to go out with my aunt instead?'

'I suppose so. That's to say, certainly. Of course.'

'Look, Fortescue! What I really – I mean to say – Well, I expect you have a notion of what's in my head? Can I come over and talk to you soon?'

'Yes, naturally. At any time. Perhaps towards the end of next week.'

'But Fortescue – '

'I'd say it needs thinking about, Comberford. There's Mrs Minton, you know. I might be put in a delicate position. But the real fact is that Evadne – ' Fortescue's voice hesitated. He appeared to be having one of his fits of maximum embarrassment. 'You see, Evadne's a – ' He broke off altogether.

'What's that?'

'Nothing, my dear fellow. Or not now.'

'You were saying something about Evadne.'

'Evadne? Oh, yes. Still in a good deal of discomfort. Frightfully nice of you to inquire. Goodbye.'

This time there was a click in the receiver. Captain Fortescue had hung up. Gadberry had a momentary vision of him at the other end of the line, mopping his brow with a large silk handkerchief. It was unsatisfactory and puzzling. But what he himself had to remember, of course, was the odd fact that, in the marriage market, he was a very big catch indeed. And Fortescue's curious staving-off tactics were simply a reflection of his almost aggressive honesty. If his daughter married the heir of Bruton it wouldn't be because her father had in any way angled for it.

Yes, that was it.

22

A distressing restlessness overtook Gadberry as the morning wore on. After his unproductive telephone conversation with Captain Fortescue he had made his way back to his own apartments with some idea of putting in a little overdue application to the *Memoirs* of Magnus Minton. If he was going to hang on – and the new world into which he had entered with Evadne made it essential that he should do so – he must maintain and strengthen his grip on the material upon which the whole colourability of his enterprise had been based. The very fact that he was now to be in constant association with two people who knew him to be an impostor was bound, he realised, to impose an additional strain on his nerve – however much, for their own ends, these two people were committed to supporting his imposture. He must do his daily prep.

This morning, however, he found it impossible to concentrate upon the endless domestic twaddle which constituted the greater part of these dreary manuscript journals. He thrust them away, and prowled broodingly round his so-called office. The prospect from its windows wasn't inspiriting. Snow was still falling – and so thickly that there occurred to him for the first time the mildly alarming thought that the whole place might soon be cut off for days or weeks. Still, the falls were continuing to be only intermittent, and when he looked up at the sky he saw signs of a break in the clouds from which they were descending. Things might cheer up a little in the afternoon.

He didn't want to smoke, and at this early hour he wouldn't allow himself to drink. He had no impulse to settle down with an improving, or even with an entertaining, book. It suddenly came to him that the life he had planned for himself at Bruton – or rather that the real Comberford had planned for him – was an awkwardly empty one. He wouldn't really ever get into the way of all that country gentleman stuff. Of course this made the transforming arrival of Evadne all the more miraculous, since in the mere contemplation of such a girl whose lifetimes could be passed in ecstasy.

Yet at the moment, somehow, even this wasn't quite working. His restlessness was mounting, so that the room had become too small to contain it. He went into the corridor, and began a kind of caged up-and-down in that. It was a narrow corridor, and quite surprisingly long. The effect was claustrophobic – rather as in one of those interminable passages in the bowels of an ocean liner. On the one side were sparely spaced lancet windows so slit-like that one had to suppose them originally constructed with some defensive intention. On the other side was that succession of forbidding cells which had constituted the surprisingly extensive penal establishment of the monastery. Some of them were gained through apertures upon which there remained no more than the stump of a rusted iron hinge. Others had massive oaken doors, iron bound and with formidable bolts. These could hardly have survived, Gadberry imagined, since before the dissolution of these monstrous monkeries by Henry VIII. Presumably they had been restored by some eighteenth-century Minton, agreeably anxious to recreate the mediaeval amenities of his residence. There would be mad monks as well as bad ones, Gadberry supposed, and they would all alike have been encouraged, when undergoing incarceration, to bang themselves with stones and wallop themselves with nettles. The dimensions of the individual cells, he reflected, must have been calculated to give elbow room, and no more, to these and other vigorous expressions of the theory of mortification and penance. High up in its outer wall, each cell had a window, if it could be called that, about large enough to admit a bat, or conceivably a member of one of the smaller species of the Abbey's owls. Apart from the abbot's lodging, it was all at a marked remove from any other part of the Abbey. It didn't seem to have been the idea that the howlings of the flagellated sinners should audibly counterpoint with the chantings of the righteous in the Abbey church and its ancillary oratories.

In such gloomy investigations and morbid reveries Gadberry found that he had wasted quite a lot of time. But in the interval, he noticed, external nature had a little cheered up. It had stopped snowing, and there was even a hint of struggling sunlight in the sky to the south. If anything, however, this only increased his restlessness, and it didn't notably alleviate his morbidity of mind. From his bedroom window he could just glimpse the tower, and he presently found himself peering out at it in a compulsive way. He had never climbed it. Did Mrs Minton ever climb it? Was Miss Bostock, binoculars over her shoulder, climbing it now? Could Boulter be made to climb it? How hazardous was the climb with all this snow and ice around? None of these questions held any significance for anything that Gadberry was proposing to do. He had already settled pretty clearly with himself just where the boundary between fantasy and actuality lay in that particular direction. Still, he would go and have a look. There could be no harm in that.

He took his own field glasses. They had belonged to Great-uncle Magnus, and although bulky were superb. It was vaguely in his head that he wanted to determine just what, apart from hawks and hernshaws, Miss Bostock in her familiar eyrie could survey when similarly accommodated herself. He walked down to the calefactory for his gumboots and duffel coat, and went outside. There was a thin wind before which the surface snow was gently drifting. But it wasn't blowing so as to add in any degree to the hazards of his climb.

The snow hadn't ceased before obliterating every minor boundary. The big formal garden still stood between its forbidding walls of cypress, but the intricate geometry of its beds and paths was concealed beneath an unbroken texture of white. And so with the great parterre dropping in shallow terraces to the fishpond. And those peripheral parts of the vast complex of buildings that had been reduced to vestigial walls from which the whole ground-plan could still be traced: these had vanished too, so that the total spectacle appeared curiously contracted or reduced. It was as if Bruton Abbey, conscious of the approaching grip of an iron winter, was curling in upon itself for survival. The effect was also curiously disorienting. Small, familiar landmarks having vanished, you could unthinkingly stray around in a disconcerting manner. Gadberry remarked this. It didn't occur to him as significant.

Nave and transepts, choir and Lady-chapel: in all of them the vaulting still stood – and with, above it, one didn't know how many tons and tons of lead. The lead couldn't conceivably go back beyond the Reformation; like much else about the Abbey, it must be the fruit of eighteenth-century eccentricity and eighteenth-century aristocratic affluence. But the vaulting had been set there by the first master builders; it had neither fallen down nor been quarried in. In his *Memoirs*, indeed, Magnus Minton had recorded his conviction – the issue of much research – that not so much as the materials of a single pigsty had ever been filched from Bruton Abbey. This was no doubt because the Mintons (who had been handed the place by Henry himself) had been quite as convinced as their future connections the Comberfords that *Hold Everything* is an excellent motto to possess. As a consequence, the place was pretty well unique in England. It was a circumstance of which Gadberry was becoming rather proud.

The clustered pillar at the north-east of the crossing had an extra girth, or rather bulge, only visible from the angle at which choir and north transept met. This allowed for a corkscrew staircase which was very dark but wholly safe. You wound your way up this, Gadberry found, for what appeared to be a very long climb indeed. This was not surprising, because when you eventually emerged in a vast, square chamber it was at a level already well above the clerestory. This had a flagged floor beneath and a raftered roof above – the latter evidently a work of pious restoration once more. Then there was another corkscrew staircase, this time much narrower, and with narrow windows at every second turn through which a whole countryside could already be glimpsed. From this you came into a second chamber, enormously high and brilliantly lit, since it was pierced on all four sides by windows which thrust staggeringly up and up through what could now be only a mere skin of stone. On one wall there was a narrow stone staircase, unguarded on its inner side, and steeply pitched so as to avoid being carried across the line of the window. It was here that you first needed a bit of nerve. Gadberry climbed cautiously – heights did a little worry him – and presently found himself, with rather staggering suddenness, in open air. He was standing on a broad, private snowfield of his own, which seemed to slope on every side from a shallow apex to a low parapet – a matter of crumbled walls rather than of contrived breastwork or crenellation – beyond which hung the absolute void. He was, he knew, a hundred and eighty feet in air – which was just half the height of the tower as it had originally stood.

He found himself looking round apprehensively for Miss Bostock. But that, of course, was absurd; there was nowhere here, as there had been nowhere on the way up, in which another human being could elude observation for an instant. This meant that the tower wasn't really a very suitable place for treble murder, or even for double or single murder, since there was no obvious way of contriving lethal ambush. But he hadn't come up here to go on elaborating that morbid sort of fantasy. Indeed, he hadn't come up here for any very particular reason at all. But at least he could focus his field glasses and take a good look round.

The river had virtually disappeared, and he now understood the explanation of something which he had been vaguely aware of when at ground level. The Abbey was a quiet enough place, but that morning, somehow, it had seemed quieter still. And here was the reason. Normally the silence was faintly but perceptibly qualified by the flowing of the river itself. But the river was totally frozen over, and no sound came from whatever sluggish current continued to flow beneath the ice.

Because the Abbey stood by the river, and indeed spanned it, and because the dales rose in a gentle swell on either side, it was only up and down the valley of the Brut that one commanded a really distant prospect even from this height. Gadberry's first impulse, inevitably, was to direct his glasses in the direction of that sacred dwelling in which his divine Evadne reposed like a pearl within its shell. Turning that way, then, as resistlessly as a compass-needle to the north, he gazed long and ardently at whatever was revealed. But the shrine, alas, lay hopelessly occluded behind the plantation that straddled the valley. He could only fancy that he just discerned a thin wisp of smoke from an invisible chimney. Perhaps, he thought tenderly, it came from some blessed fire kindled in his beloved's bedroom. But then the image of her immaculate body lying there, cruelly maimed (for in such perfection even a fractured or sprained ankle must count as maiming) and patiently suffering: this vision was too much to bear; the marvellous clarity and definition of Great-uncle Magnus' binoculars was suddenly impaired by a watery suffusion; Gadberry had to dry his tears before turning away and directing his curiosity in the other direction.

Now, of course, he was looking at the village of Bruton. It lay in no more than the middle distance, and the glasses brought it almost disconcertingly under his nose. The effect – as often when such an instrument is used from a height – was to make him turn giddy in a very alarming way. The gently sloping sheet of snow on which he stood seemed to heave and turn. For a wild moment he thought it had become precipitous, and that he was about to tumble down it into empty space. Then this disagreeable sensation passed. He saw that he was looking at a Bruton vicarage which was slowly stabilising itself, like a ship coming on an even keel amid some subsiding swell.

The large and hideous house could not all be brought into focus at once. At the moment – just as if he were about to pay a visit there – he was looking straight at its front door. He could see, quite distinctly, the bell at which he had vainly tugged while the Reverend Mr Grimble – but had it been Grimble? – had peered at him from an upper window. It was a sinister and displeasing recollection. He had almost forgotten, in the immediate press of his affairs at the Abbey, that this disreputable clerical conjuror had revealed a kind of gleeful hostility towards him which he had found quite upsetting at the time. And this discomposure returned to him now. He had a sudden fantastic vision of Grimble crouched in a kind of laboratory somewhere in his rambling house, and beguiling himself by sticking pins into a wax image of himself, George Gadberry *alias* Comberford. This was very ridiculous, but it caused Gadberry to divert his binoculars away from the vicarage in order to survey its comparatively innocuous environs.

On one side lay the churchyard; on the other was a field sheltering, in a fashion, a small flock of sheep. There was nothing remarkable about the creatures – which were, after all, the commonest inhabitants of these dales. Or there was nothing remarkable about all save one. This sheep – and it appeared a very large specimen – was in some way out of focus. It appeared, at least, to be moving on an odd plane as compared with the others. And the reason for this was apparent almost as soon as Gadberry had noticed it. This sheep wasn't in the field at all. It was on the flat roof of an outbuilding contiguous with the vicarage.

Gadberry found this surprising. He was not, it was true, a countryman. Had the aberrant sheep been a goat he would probably have told himself that there was nothing improbable in its having achieved such a scramble. But sheep, he was tolerably sure, seldom scale roofs – even flat ones. Nor – he now added to himself – do they commonly move in quite the way this sheep was moving.

The sheep proceeded with a curious effect of caution across the roof, and towards the wall of the main vicarage building which abutted on it. The sheep approached a window. Even more cautiously, the sheep nosed at this window. It then raised a sash, and disappeared inside.

What might have been termed a dim and undetermined sense of unknown modes of being descended upon Gadberry for a while. The sight he had just witnessed was something monstrous and unnatural. For some moments he gropingly connected it with the reprehensible magical practices of the Vicar of Bruton; this sheep was not really a sheep; it was some ghastly familiar – a fiend, so to speak, in sheep's clothing.

But this extravagant speculation didn't last for long. Gadberry bore, after all, a tolerably rational mind. He quickly told himself that there was a simpler explanation of the sheep's sneaking in through that window. The sheep wasn't a sheep at all. It was a human being in some bulky and light-coloured raincoat or the like. And it had presented the form it did because creeping on hands and knees. Somebody was making a distinctly covert exploration of the Reverend Mr Grimble's abode. He himself needed only a little patience to discover who that somebody was.

He remained with his glasses trained upon the window. It had been lowered again gently from within. Perhaps that was to prevent some telltale draught from blowing through the vicarage. But it struck Gadberry as an action which only an intruder with a pretty steady nerve would take. He continued to wait. He waited so long that he was on the verge of concluding the whole thing to have been nonsense – a mere hallucination bred of the constant agitations to which his life was at present exposed.

And then the window went up again. The sheep emerged, and stood up boldly on two feet. The sheep raised its head, and contrived an uncanny effect of gazing direct, and seeingly, into Gadberry's eyes. Gadberry was only too familiar with that straight look. The sheep was Miss Bostock.

23

Gadberry came down from the tower in a mood of sober thought. There was nothing freakish about Miss Bostock – as there was (say) about himself, or about the real Nicholas Comberford (as he supposed), or about the necromantic Mr Grimble. Miss Bostock was simply a very unscrupulous and ruthless woman, who had seen through a fantastic deception, and who was determined to exploit the resulting situation to her own ends. And she was an efficient person, so that it was a reasonable bet that her entire concentration was being devoted to the job she had taken on. She hadn't, therefore, gone spying at the vicarage at the prompting of any trivial and extraneous curiosity. She had done so because Grimble – Grimble in some relationship or another – had his place right at the heart of the matter.

Grimble had at least one visitor, one house-guest, at the vicarage. At least one person had arrived unobtrusively, locked away a car in a hurry, bolted into the house, and thereafter remained invisible. Miss Bostock had been aware of Gadberry's own call at the vicarage. She had enjoyed, in fact, at that time, precisely the same close-up and telescopic view of the place as Gadberry himself had just been doing. *She* had seen that odd arrival too. It was what she had been further exploring, with characteristic enterprise and resolution, when she had slipped (like a sheep into the fold, so to speak) through that upper window.

Were the present a narrative conducted upon philosophic principles, or dedicated to the unravelling of intricate states of mind, it would be necessary to pause at this point in an attempt to determine whether Gadberry, as he contemplated these facts, became – obscurely, subliminally, subconsciously, or unconsciously – possessed of a substantial part of the true state of the case. Certainly a great deal was going to happen – and happen very soon – which was to have the appearance of surprising and confounding him utterly. But the possibility cannot be excluded – and one need say no more than this – that in some confused part of his head he was not hopelessly behind the reader in his sense of what was really going on. If he appears – again at this point – to be distinctly on the thick side, we may (if we want to be charitable) attribute this to the obfuscating effect of a further and utterly obliterating fall of snow. Down it came again – and much as if it had hardly been in earnest until this moment. Far from finding his way securely through his appalling predicament, he had a good deal of difficulty in even finding his way back to the house. At one point, indeed, he walked straight across the fishpond – and almost fell through one of the holes that would have companioned him with the pike.

This new blizzard had one important consequence. By the middle of the afternoon, it became absolutely clear that the call upon the Shilbottles could not take place. Indeed, Lady Arthur was thoughtful enough to ring up with the news that her drive was totally blocked, and that it would remain so until snowploughs had operated in a big way. This telephone call was the last that came through to the Abbey. Nor could any more go out. As was customary in that part of Yorkshire under these disagreeable climatic conditions, the lines were down.

But if one couldn't drive to the Shilbottles, one could certainly walk to the Fortescues. Any resolute lover would have been convinced of this, and Gadberry was certainly a resolute lover. It would take a certain amount of time, and quite a lot of effort. If he didn't arrive exhausted, he would at least arrive looking pretty adequately exercised. And this ought to gain him merit – he couldn't help thinking – when he did that job of sinking down on his knees by the bedside of his beloved.

So he set off down the drive. He was almost at once surprised by how heavy the going actually was. Every step forward involved tugging a foot out of from six to eighteen inches of snow, and quite soon the effort appeared to be telling not only on his legs but right up his back as well. He slowed his pace. To stride in breathed and glowing would be one thing, to stagger in puffed and sweating would be quite another. It was a further instance of the formidable character of Miss Bostock, it occurred to him, that she had made her own reconnaissance of the vicarage in face of these conditions.

It had stopped snowing, and the sky was blowing clear. With surprising speed the solid and louring cloud-ceiling had broken up, and now great chunks and streamers of it were in rapid movement. The effect of this was to make Gadberry's own progress appear yet more plodding. But the effect was exhilarating as well. It was some time before he noticed how much the snow was in answering movement. It was being blown – preponderantly in his own direction, but in whirls and eddies as well – across its own surface like a fine smoke. If this went on, there would be tremendous drifts by morning.

Eventually he reached the spot where he had heard Evadne's anguished cry. Eager though he was to press forward, he nevertheless paused, scrambled over the familiar dyke, and reverently surveyed the sacred ground. It was rather, of course, the sacred snow – and so much more had fallen that no trace remained of Evadne's ski-tracks or her recumbent form. The skis, he supposed, were still buried here. They must be rescued – for were they not to be his cherished possession forever?

Heartened and refreshed, he went on his way. It was still daylight, but he wasn't going to have very long with Evadne if he was to get back to the Abbey before dusk – and under present conditions being overtaken by the deeper shades of evening, let alone by darkness, mightn't be fun. So he pushed up the pace again, and soon he had only a few hundred yards to go.

Hitherto the only sound had been his own breathing and the crunch of his boots. But now the snow was beginning to whistle and whisper as it sifted beneath the wind. He was listening to this when he suddenly realised that he was listening to something else too. There were voices ahead of him – excited voices – and then shouts of laughter. He turned a corner, and the house was before him, beyond a small paddock in which the snow was everywhere trodden vigorously underfoot. Three young people were skylarking in it: a boy whom Gadberry recognised as Evadne's younger brother; a second boy of about the same age, who looked as if he might be the gardener's son; and a rather older girl. All three were racing about madly, bombarding each other with snowballs, joining or separating in strategic rushes, and yelling at one another like fiends. The girl took a tumble as Gadberry watched. She was up again and running in a flash, making a grab, as she did so, at a little fur hat which had fallen from her head. It was a head that now showed in a glory of golden hair. The girl was Evadne herself.

For a single and unspeakable moment Gadberry's heart was filled with joy. Evadne's injury had vanished, miraculously cured. And then – in a single answering instant – the truth rushed upon him and overwhelmed him. No sprained ankle ever behaves like that. Evadne Fortescue was a fraud.

You see, Evadne's a – The embarrassed voice of Captain Fortescue on the telephone, beginning thus before seeming to lose the will to communicate, came clearly back to Gadberry now. *You see, Evadne's a little bitch.* Perhaps the completed sentence would have been that. Or perhaps *bitch* would have been *fraud* or *schemer* of even *fortune hunter.* It didn't much matter which. The ski accident had been a fake. The girl had lain in wait and rigged it, knowing that Gadberry was coming that way.

Had Gadberry been a moral giant, he might himself have filled his arms with snowballs, and advanced laughing upon the guilty scene. As it was, he turned and stumbled blindly away. His passion had been instantaneous and romantic. His disillusionment was instantaneous too, and very bitter indeed. He might be compared (entirely adequately) to one of those unfortunate heroes of Thomas Hardy's, whom some ingenious irony of circumstance clobbers pretty well into the dust. Gadberry, of course, was clobbered into snow. The stuff seemed twice as deep as it had been only a couple of minutes before. In no time at all, he felt that he had been walking round and round in it for hours.

Later, this is what he *had* been doing. His shattered retreat from the treacherous and Circean dwelling of the Fortescues must have been in the wrong direction. There was no track under his feet; there was no landmark within his vision. Had he been disposed to cry out, with Goethe's tedious Faust, *Wohin der Weg?* he would undoubtedly have received as answer the Mephistophelean *Kein Weg! Ins Unbetretene.* Shelter of a sort did, however, eventually receive him. Finding himself sitting before a tolerable fire, and with a glass of whisky in his hand, he dimly concluded that he must have found his way to some lone alehouse in the Yorkshire moors.

It was while thus circumstanced that the scales fell from George Gadberry's eyes. Evadne Fortescue had pretended to be what she was not: a maiden in distress, and one quite fortuitously succoured by a knight-errant chancing to pass that way. In contriving this imposture, Evadne had inflicted upon a fellow human being outrageous and immeasurable pain. It was clear, therefore, that all deliberate deception must be wrong. And must be quite *absolutely* wrong. His own deception had been precisely that.

Gadberry finished his whisky, paid for it, and made careful inquiries about the direction in which Bruton Abbey lay. It was his business to return there, and to confess to Mrs Minton.

24

But Mrs Minton had gone to bed. Realising that it was really as late as that, Gadberry understood that he must in fact have wandered around in a state of shock for quite some time. He was very tired, and he wasn't at all hungry. Boulter, however, insisted on serving him a meal of some elaboration. It was a succession of depressingly chilly dishes – Boulter referred to it as a cold collation – which Gadberry endeavoured, not perhaps wholly judiciously, to render more digestible by the concomitance of several glasses of claret. There was no need to keep absolutely sober. Mrs Minton had given directions that she was to be informed immediately upon his safe return (his absence, naturally, having caused concern) but that she was not to be otherwise disturbed. He could hardly break into her bedchamber with his shocking avowal, so it would have to keep till the morning. He himself might be in better trim to go through with it then.

'And now,' Gadberry said to Boulter, 'I'm going to bed.' It is possible that he spoke a little roughly. Boulter's continuing to keep up a bogus and butler-like distance was coming to annoy him very much.

'Very good, sir. You will no doubt wish to be called at the usual hour. Before you retire, may I venture to inquire into the nature of your occasions this afternoon?'

'No. You may not.'

'Indeed, sir?' Boulter's eyebrows hitched themselves slightly aloft on his impassive face. 'May I venture to suggest the desirability of a relation of confidence continuing to subsist between us?'

'Go to hell, Boulter.' Gadberry produced this quite pleasantly. 'And stay there. See?'

There was a moment's silence. Boulter replaced the claret jug thoughtfully on the sideboard. Then he took a long look at Gadberry – a look that would have done justice to Miss Bostock herself.

'Young man,' he said, 'you had better keep a civil tongue in your head.'

Gadberry laughed aloud. It was something he had expected never to do again. But at last Boulter was looking ugly, and this was a great satisfaction to him.

'Boulter,' he said, 'you've had it. Before you go to bed, I advise you to put in a quiet hour packing your bags. I shall be doing just that myself.'

Boulter – and this was more satisfactory still – turned from pink to purple between his butler's regulation mutton-chop whiskers.

'You young twister!' he gasped. 'If you think you can – '

'As it happens, I do. I think *just* that. And it means you've had it. See? You've proposed to conspire with a young twister against a generous employer who puts implicit trust in your loyalty.' Gadberry felt a real access of righteous indignation as he delivered himself of this. 'You haven't a chance of keeping your job. Not a dog's, puppy's, kitten's, or furry caterpillar's chance. Good night.'

And Gadberry rose and walked from the room – wearily, but with the sense of one good job done. With Miss Bostock, he hoped, there would be a repeat performance next day.

The walk – it might almost be called the journey – to his own quarters seemed interminable. In the cloisters a casement window was swinging to and fro on creaking hinges; it must have been blown open by the rising wind. And a rising wind, once more, there certainly was. It was beginning to put on its howling act. Against this, the senior resident owl (as it probably was) had started to complain. Gadberry paused for a moment to listen to this dismal dialogue.

It was the owl that shriek'd, the fatal bellman
Which gives the stern'st good-night...

He was through, thank goodness, with all that Thane of Cawdor stuff.

A staircase, a corridor, a staircase: all empty and very cold. And then his own corridor. He had come to think of it as that. But it was as dreary as the rest of the place. He saw no reason to suppose that any of Her Majesty's prisons would be notably drearier. Through the long row of lancet windows there came an odd effect as of a very faint lightning operating in slow motion. The sky had continued to clear. There was a gibbous moon in it, and across this the last of the storm-clouds were racing. In the corridor there was no more than a faint light outside his rooms at the far end, so this eerie flickering had it all its own way. His own shadow came and went oddly. In front of him one of the massive cell doors swung half open. He had never seen that happen before, even in as high a wind as the one now rising.

This was the thought in Gadberry's mind when something black and sweet-smelling was clapped over his face. He felt his legs melt beneath him. And then he passed out.

He came to slowly, and at first to no more than a consciousness that the world was revolving round him as if he were the notional centre of a top. Then with a jar like the sudden application of a powerful brake this sensation vanished, to be replaced by the astonishing discovery that he was tied up. His wrists were bound behind him; his ankles were bound; he was slumped on a floor with his shoulders against a wall.

Gadberry had often read of this sort of thing happening. It is a commonplace in certain types of romance. The victims are invariably confident they will get free again, and they always start using their wits at once. Gadberry found that he hadn't any wits. He was aware of nothing except terror. In this helpless posture anybody could do anything to him. The thought was unbearable.

'Well, that's stage one.'

The voice came as from a great distance. It was cheerful, and might even have been called friendly. Gadberry closed his eyes for a moment and then opened them – suddenly determined at least not to be too frightened to *see*. He was in a corner of one of the cells. There was some light from a small electric torch in the middle of the floor.

'That's right,' said the voice. 'Take a good look round. My guess is that it's tolerably like something you'll be becoming pretty familiar with.'

Gadberry's glance had been on an indefinably sinister-looking black bag in a corner of the cell. Now he turned his head painfully towards the voice. Very oddly, somebody appeared to have brought a looking-glass into the place too. That could be the only explanation of the fact that he was staring at his own face. And then, in a flash, he realised the truth. What he was looking at was the face of the real Nicholas Comberford.

He was so astounded that his fear left him. His mind even began faintly to function again. Whatever devilry Comberford was up to, it wasn't likely to run to unspeakable physical outrage. The man was no doubt in some sense mad. But he wasn't an absolute maniac. He could even be conversed with.

'Where on earth have *you* come from?' Gadberry asked.

Comberford laughed. He appeared to find this opening amusing.

'Well,' he said, 'at the moment just from the vicarage. You almost saw me arriving there.'

'I did see you. Only I didn't know who it was.'

'That was too bad. It's a convenient base. And old Grimble is a convenient spy. I know things about him, you see, that he wouldn't like bruited abroad. Besides, he likes mischief for its own sake.'

'I know all that. Look here, Comberford, you'd better stop this imbecile fooling, and untie me at once. The whole thing has been utterly idiotic from the start.'

'Has it? I don't know that I agree. It's satisfactory, isn't it, that the old woman has signed on those dotted lines?'

'I don't care a damn for her dotted lines.'

'No more you should, old boy. They're no concern of yours now. It's curtains for Gadberry, you know. Of course, it's curtains for the old girl too.'

'What do you mean?' This time, Gadberry had difficulty in getting the words out. His terror had returned. It was a physical thing, running in cold drops down his spine.

'I don't know that I've any call to tell you. Still, you might as well know – if only by way of passing the time.' Comberford paused to glance at his watch. 'Yes, better give them another half-hour. Or even an hour. There's no hurry. I can't, in any event, get away until the small hours. You yourself will require my individual attention again round about two o'clock.'

This time, Gadberry felt a horrible sensation at the roots of his hair. Even to repeat 'What do you mean?' was beyond him. He stared at Comberford dumbly.

'Drugs are tricky things,' Comberford said. 'Particularly if all we want to suggest is a fellow who has lost his nerve and got hopelessly tight. And we mustn't, of course, risk your recovering any control of yourself until the cops are on the spot and ready to collect. That means – as I say – giving you the final shot round about two. The snow's the only worry. It may make things a little awkward. Still, I'm pretty securely in the South of France, you know. So nothing much can go wrong.' Comberford fell silent. He seemed indisposed to talk more after all.

'I wonder whether you've thought out all the details,' Gadberry said. 'Elaborate crimes usually go wrong. If you were as clever as you think you are, you'd have thought of something a damned sight simpler.'

'I might beguile the odd half-hour kicking you, or something like that.' Comberford was clearly offended. 'What about it, old boy?'

'Don't be silly. Bruises would wreck your whole crackpot scheme. By the way, I think these cords, or whatever they are, are going to do that anyway. By the feel of them, they've raised weals already. What will your precious cops make of *that*?'

'Damnation!' Comberford was plainly startled. But then he recovered himself and grinned. 'Do you know,' he said, 'that it's uncommonly obliging of you to point that out? I'll ease them for a bit. But lie down on your stomach, and then don't move.'

Gadberry obeyed this order. He concluded, as he felt the bonds slacken, that he had won a first trick. Those on his ankles would need untying before he could stand up. But he believed that, at a pinch, he could now free his wrists with a quick twist.

'That shows,' he said, without raising his head from the floor. 'Detail's not your strong point – Comberford, old boy.'

'Listen. I leave you here. I smother the old woman – '

'Smother her, do you? What rot!'

'Yes, I do. It's going to look like a very clumsy attempt to suggest natural death in her sleep – heart-failure, or something like that. I take care to leave in her room certain tokens of your own presence, dear boy – I won't tell you what. I come back here and give you your shots. I bundle you into your own room, get a good deal of whisky into your stomach – and that's that. That's the whole thing, and I depart from the dear old Abbey as I came. The body is found, the doctor comes, the police come, they pay you a not very polite call – and there you are, still snoring like a pig.'

> *I'll gild the faces of the grooms withal,*
> *For it must seem their guilt...*

The icy drops were coursing down Gadberry's spine once more. This time, they seemed each to explode with a tiny splash deep in his loins. He had been rash to think that the world of *Macbeth* was safely behind him.

'It won't do *you* any good,' he said. 'It just can't.'

Comberford looked at his watch again.

'Don't be silly,' he said. 'In my little Riviera nest – where I have a cast-iron alibi now – the sad news of this foul deed reaches me. I turn up. I have reason to suspect, I say, that a letter written to me by my great-aunt some months ago was intercepted. And intercepted by *you*, old boy. There's a story waiting to make a plausible job of that. You turned up at the Abbey. You waited – and only just waited – until the will and what not were signed – '

'You bloody fool!' Risking something unpleasant, Gadberry rolled over on his back. 'You don't think those precious documents will be valid, do you?'

'Of course they'll be valid, old boy. The impostor is out of the picture – hanged or at least jugged for good. But the heir remains the man intended: the authentic Nicholas Comberford. And that's me. I get what I've always meant to get – without ever coming near this place, and without waiting until the old girl *does* die a natural death – at about a hundred and two. It's in the bag, George my lad. It's all in the beautiful bag.'

'*I think not.*'

Suddenly, there was another and more powerful torch at play in the cell. It was in the left hand of Miss Bostock, who stood in the door. In her right hand there was a gun.

25

'May I introduce you to Miss Bostock?' Gadberry said. At the same time he gave a quick tug at his wrists. He had been right. They came free quite easily. He sat up, stretched his arms – it was already a painful process – and untied the knots at his ankles. Nobody hindered him. Comberford and Miss Bostock were too much at gaze, so to speak, to notice. Gadberry contented himself with wriggling into a corner in his sitting posture, and there a little taking his ease. He had a notion that the situation remained on the tricky side.

'An *embarras de richesses*,' Miss Bostock said. 'One Nicholas Comberford too many. The question is, which is to survive? Perhaps we might hold an auction. No – don't move.' She had said this in response to a threatening gesture by Comberford. 'Unless you want the problem resolved out of hand.'

'*Permit me, madam.*'

With the effect of a conjuring trick, a dark-sleeved arm had appeared behind Miss Bostock, and the small pistol had been snatched from her hand. In the same moment she was given a not very respectful impetus from behind – indeed, on the behind, and from a powerful knee. She was thus jolted into the cell. And Boulter was commanding it from the doorway.

'All the conspirators,' Gadberry said. For *Macbeth* was out. It seemed reasonable to switch to *Julius Caesar*.

Or even – Gadberry was to reflect afterwards – to *A Comedy of Errors* or *All's Well that Ends Well*. Abruptly, that is to say, the situation had modulated into the absurd. Unfortunately, as it turned out, nobody except himself appeared aware of this possible change of key.

His three companions were glaring at each other – and at him, for that matter – with undisguised malignity. As it was, he made one forlorn gesture in the direction of a certain lightness of air.

'Couldn't we,' he asked, 'have Grimble along? It would seem the tidy thing to do.'

'I've got the gun,' Boulter said.

'You have, indeed.' Miss Bostock simultaneously recovered her physical equilibrium and her nervous poise. 'Only, it isn't loaded.'

There was a pregnant silence, while Boulter verified this. The stillness was broken only by the flapping of an intrusive bat. From somewhere outside – perhaps from the tower itself – one of the resident owls hooted. It was on a satirical note.

'Thank you, madam.' Boulter handed the useless weapon back to its owner. He had returned to his most wooden manner. 'It would appear that some accommodation must be arrived at.'

'Accommodation to hell,' Gadberry said – still from his seat on the floor. 'From now on it's going to be the truth.' He glanced at each of his companions in turn. 'The whole bloody truth, and nothing but the bloody truth,' he added by way of emphasis.

Miss Bostock looked at him coldly.

'Young man,' she said, 'for I don't know your name –'

'His name,' Comberford said, 'is –'

'You shut your mouth,' Gadberry said. This injunction, although crudely expressed, appeared to carry weight, at least for the time. Comberford fell warily silent.

'Young man,' Miss Bostock resumed, 'that was a very foolish remark. The truth is a luxury to be afforded by none of us. By you least of all.'

Gadberry stretched himself. He was still feeling uncomfortably stiff. He chafed his wrists, and then chafed his ankles.

'That's certainly true of Comberford,' he said. 'He has been lurking in the vicarage. He has been plotting with the old imbecile Grimble, who wouldn't stand up to police interrogation for ten minutes. He has broken into the Abbey in the night. In that black bag he has chloroform, other soporific drugs and – if I have understood him aright – a hypodermic syringe. He's for it.'

'And what about you?' Still blocking the doorway, Boulter produced this with one of his abrupt returns to the natural man. 'You've lived here under false pretences for months. *You're* for it, you young bastard, if anybody is.'

'But the point about me is that I don't mind.' Gadberry stood up. 'Can you get that into your thick skull? *I don't mind.*'

There was another silence – rather a long one, this time. Everybody seemed to be paying this the compliment of rather serious attention. Then Miss Bostock spoke. It was with an air of patiently beginning again from rational premises.

'It appears to me that the superfluous person is the real Mr Comberford. Until his arrival, we were getting on very well. Boulter and I, it is true, were a little in the dark about each other. But our interests are readily reconcilable.'

'That's right!' Boulter nodded his head vigorously 'Our money's on the fake Comberford, not the true one.' He paused as if to consider. 'Could this chap – the real Comberford – *prove* himself to be the real Comberford? That's the point. If he couldn't – '

'Of course he could.' Miss Bostock was impatient. 'And any dispute about identity would be fatal. Start investigating our own young man's claim, and it wouldn't stand up for a week. Probably not for a day.'

'Then, in that case, there seems to be only one thing for it.' Boulter eyed Comberford grimly before turning back to Miss Bostock. 'Don't you agree?'

'Certainly I agree. One regrets the necessity. But it is self evident.'

'It's unfortunate the ground's so hard.'

'Yes – but other means can be thought of.'

At this moment – rather unexpectedly and wholly fatally – the true Nicholas Comberford's nerve broke. And panic lent him strength. He took a lunge at the portly Boulter which sent him sprawling into the corridor. A split second later, he was in full flight down it himself.

Calmly scrutinised, this precipitate retreat might have yielded much that was rational. There was nothing more in Bruton Abbey for Nicholas Comberford; in that direction he had dished himself for good. He was in the presence of two baffled and ruthless antagonists, and of a man whom he had proposed to see indicted of murder. To cut his losses and stand not upon the order of his going was sensible enough.

But there was really nothing rational about the pursuit. It was a matter of sheer confusion, and perhaps of something like blood-lust. Strangely enough, Miss Bostock led it – and at a speed which might have been envied by Atalanta, or by swift Camilla scouring the plain. Boulter followed, cursing and looking round for a weapon as he ran. Gadberry, utterly astonished by this fantastic rout, at first brought up the rear. Surely they couldn't really intend – He decided to suspend speculation, and crowd on speed.

Corridor, staircase, corridor, staircase. Cloisters, abbot's arch, scriptorium, monks' arch. Strangers' hall, locutory, gatehouse. They all went past as in a dream. The chase was now in open air. The wind still whistled, and it was bringing up more clouds heavy with snow from the north. But to the south the moon still flicked in and out of mere shreds and patches, so that the Abbey with its ruins and its gardens, its fishpond and its terraced parterre, was behaving like an ancient and decomposing film. Amid all this, Comberford was a dark, headlong blotch on the snow.

'Comberford, stop! Stop, you fool!' Gadberry spared breath to yell thus desperately, for he had suddenly realised the fantastic hazard ahead. But it was in vain. The fleeing man, wholly disoriented, had steered a course straight across the fishpond. And the thousand-to-one chance fulfilled itself. There was a quite small sound – rather like the plop of a frog in a stream. Nicholas Comberford had vanished. His inheritance at Bruton was with its pike.

For a long time Gadberry knelt by the dark hole – the other two standing silent beside him. But there was nothing whatever to be done. Finally he got to his feet.

'We make a bargain,' he said.

'A bargain? What do you mean?' Boulter spoke aggressively, but there was uncertainty in his tone.

'We let each other alone. I'm going – now, this minute. You return to the house. You get rid of Comberford's bag. You find the hat I've been wearing lately – the deerstalker. You leave it here by the hole. When the body's found – which won't be for some time – it will be *my* body.'

'Your body?' Miss Bostock said.

'Damn it, woman, you know what I mean. It will be the body of the only Nicholas Comberford to have been at the Abbey for years. He behaved pretty crazily this afternoon; he went wandering out again tonight and had this ghastly accident. One of you can get that car away from the vicarage – and that buttons it up. There may be odds and ends.' He looked at Miss Bostock. 'But they're not beyond your wits to get away with. And you're lucky, both of you. So is poor old Aunt Prudence, if she only knew it. She's got rid of two rotten great-nephews at one go. Goodbye.'

The first flakes of the next snowstorm were beginning to eddy in the wind. By morning they would have obliterated all traces of this wild chase. And they had an immediate utility now. George Gadberry, with fifteen pounds in his pocket and a lesson in his head, made a moderately dramatic exit through their gentle fall.

Michael Innes

Appleby At Allington

Sir John Appleby dines one evening at Allington Park, the Georgian home of his acquaintance, Owain Allington, who is new to the area. His curiosity is aroused when Allington mentions his nephew and heir to the estate, Martin Allington, whose name Appleby recognises. The evening comes to an end but, just as Appleby is leaving, they find a dead man – electrocuted in the *son et lumière* box that had been installed in the grounds.

Appleby On Ararat

Inspector Appleby is stranded on a very strange island, with a rather odd bunch of people – too many men, too few women (and one of them too attractive) cause a deal of trouble. But that is nothing compared to later developments, including the body afloat in the water and the attack by local inhabitants.

'Every sentence he writes has flavour, every incident flamboyance'
– *Times Literary Supplement*

MICHAEL INNES

THE DAFFODIL AFFAIR

Inspector Appleby's aunt is most distressed when her horse, Daffodil – a somewhat half-witted animal with exceptional numerical skills – goes missing from her stable in Harrogate. Meanwhile, Hudspith is hot on the trail of Lucy Rideout, an enigmatic young girl who has been whisked away to an unknown isle by a mysterious gentleman. And when a house in Bloomsbury, supposedly haunted, also goes missing, the baffled policemen search for a connection. As Appleby and Hudspith trace Daffodil and Lucy, the fragments begin to come together and an extravagant project is uncovered, leading them to a South American jungle.

'Yet another surprising firework display of wit and erudition and ingenious invention'
– *Guardian*

DEATH AT THE PRESIDENT'S LODGING

Inspector Appleby is called to St Anthony's College, where the President has been murdered in his Lodging. Scandal abounds when it becomes clear that the only people with any motive to murder him are the only people who had the opportunity – because the President's Lodging opens off Orchard Ground, which is locked at night, and only the Fellows of the College have keys…

'It is quite the most accomplished first crime novel that I have read…all first-rate entertainment'
– Cecil Day Lewis, *Daily Telegraph*

Michael Innes

Hamlet, Revenge!

At Seamnum Court, seat of the Duke of Horton, The Lord Chancellor of England is murdered at the climax of a private presentation of *Hamlet*, in which he plays Polonius. Inspector Appleby pursues some of the most famous names in the country, unearthing dreadful suspicion.

'Michael Innes is in a class by himself among writers of detective fiction' – *Times Literary Supplement*

The Long Farewell

Lewis Packford, the great Shakespearean scholar, was thought to have discovered a book annotated by the Bard – but there is no trace of this valuable object when Packford apparently commits suicide. Sir John Appleby finds a mixed bag of suspects at the dead man's house, who might all have a good motive for murder. The scholars and bibliophiles who were present might have been tempted by the precious document in Packford's possession. And Appleby discovers that Packford had two secret marriages, and that both of these women were at the house at the time of his death.

11632648R00100

Printed in Great Britain
by Amazon.co.uk, Ltd.,
Marston Gate.